Kid Palomino

By the same author

The Valko Kid

Kid Palomino

MICHAEL D. GEORGE

A Black Horse Western

ROBERT HALE · LONDON

ISBN 0 7090 6438 1

Robert Hale Limited
Clerkenwell House
Clerkenwell Green
London EC1R 0HT

Photoset in North Wales by
Derek Doyle & Associates, Mold, Flintshire.
Printed and bound in Great Britain by
WBC Book Manufacturers Limited, Bridgend

Dedicated to my children
Lucy, James, Suzi, Denis and Candice

One

The two riders came over the top of the sand-dunes before reining their mounts to a halt. The first rider sat upon a magnificent palomino stallion. The rich golden tan of its coat highlighted by its long, creamy, white mane and tail looked out of place in most of the desolate places these two riders often found themselves. This tall young man had become known over the past few years simply as 'Kid Palomino', on account of his horse. His true name had long been forgotten, by everyone except the man himself.

The second rider was less pleasing to the eye, his was a drab brown quarter-horse. Its rider was a short-in-the-leg man who seemed always to have one eye closed. Not that there was anything wrong with his vision, he just never used both eyes at the same time. His bright red beard and thinning matching hair seemed to give him the appearance of someone much older than his true age. Whatever his true age was.

The one thing these two had in common was their

speed with their six-guns. This man was known simply as 'Red Rivers'. He too had long ceased to use his original name.

The pair had met a couple of years earlier and stuck together on their endless quest across the west. They took whatever jobs they could get most of the time. They had ridden herd on trail drives and on occasions found themselves working on ranches. But mostly they had worked as lawmen. Sometimes they had been deputy US Marshals, other times they were deputy sheriffs. Now they were heading for the wide open spaces of Wyoming where they had been offered jobs in a town short of experienced law officers. It was a long ride to the Wyoming Territory. Now, as these two men were almost out of Colorado, it seemed that they had a lot of time to consider their actions.

The trail ahead was vague, due to the drifting white sand, but a long way off they could see a mountain range. That was all they required to spur their mounts onward.

Before the dust had settled behind them they had continued on toward the chilly mountains. Not that they wanted to get anywhere close to snow, but they knew that before the mountains there was a town called Badwater Creek. That, they were informed, was the last place in Colorado where they might find anything remotely resembling a town. There they would rest their mounts and get a decent meal before checking into a hotel for the night. It had been ten days since they had slept in a bed or eaten anything other than beans. Tonight they intended to mollycoddle themselves.

The pair rode for another four hours through the drifting sand at a steady pace. The sun beat down mercilessly upon their backs as they rode. This desert was soon to be replaced by the fertile valley ahead, and, beyond the tall trees, lay the remote town of Badwater Creek. You could not find this or any other town on any government maps, and the two riders only knew of its existence from the letter they had received, offering them employment in Wyoming.

Ahead of them the trail seemed to narrow and make its way through tall fir and pine trees. It would have been a perfect sight except for one thing. That one thing was smoke. Snaking its way skyward.

Kid Palomino and his partner Red Rivers drew their mounts to a halt when they noticed the smoke ahead.

About a mile before them the forest started and the grass turned from brown to a colour which was close to green. The smoke rose from beyond the tree line.

It didn't look like a forest fire to the two riders, it looked as if something man-made was alight. The smoke was black, and that usually meant painted wood burning.

Painted wood usually meant a homestead.

'What you reckon that is, Kid?' Red Rivers asked his pal as they both stood up in their stirrups, balancing by leaning against the saddle-castle, vainly trying to see further.

'Something's burning, Red,' Palomino grimaced across at his friend as he gathered in his reins.

'Smart.' Red shook his head. 'What you reckon is burning?'

'I figure a house or barn. Let's go and see.'

Kid Palomino spurred his mount and looked back at his friend as his elegant mount raced ahead.

'Come on, Red!' he yelled.

Red spurred his horse into action and started to chase the stallion. The only way he could catch his friend was if Kid Palomino allowed him to. The younger man tugged at his leather reins until his complaining companion drew level.

Both horses galloped strongly toward the area of the rising smoke as their riders gave them their heads.

The two riders left the soft sand and felt the solid ground under their horses' hooves as they closed on toward the trees and the smoke. Circling the line of tall spruce trees they hit a narrow, well-used trail.

There was a lot of smoke. Choking smoke. The blaze that came from the inferno which had once been a house was out of hand.

Both riders seemed to stop their horses at once as they reached the picket fence, which seemed to indicate that this was a smallholding of some sort. Dismounting at speed, the two men raced through the open gateway into the yard.

Red and the Kid ran quickly toward the house, but the heat of the flames pushed them back. It was hot. Terribly hot.

Palomino looked frantically around before spotting the full trough and a bucket. He pulled his friend toward it.

'What ya figuring on doing, Palomino?' Red shouted at his friend, as the younger man tossed his Stetson to the ground and dunked his head and upper body into the cold water. He picked up the bucket and soaked his pants thoroughly before heading toward the front door which was black with scorch-burns. The flames were furiously beginning to lick up the side of the panelled walls.

Kid Palomino removed his gunbelt and handed the guns to the older man.

'I'm going in!' he shouted over the roaring noise of the fire.

Before Red Rivers could say anything, his partner had rushed to the front of the house and shouldered down the door. The black smoke billowed out as the Kid rolled over the shattered wood.

It seemed like an eternity to the waiting red-haired man, as he stood holding his hand before his face, trying to stop the heat from burning his whiskers.

Then the smoke seemed to come out, along with a back-draught of flames, straight at the waiting man. Red Rivers had to jump backward as the flames fanned about his legs. Inside the funnel of smoke was his partner Palomino, who rolled across the ground

11

at Red's feet. The Kid held tightly onto a young woman in his arms. She was black with soot that had deposited itself onto her face and clothing. Parts of her dress were alight, and Red stomped out the flames.

Red Rivers dashed over to the trough and filled the bucket up with the cold water. On returning, he threw the contents over the two people, who lay at his feet on the ground, gasping for clean air. The water seemed to help both parties as they somehow staggered upright, coughing. The Kid grabbed the young female's small hand and led her away from the unbearable heat of the blazing house, before finding a cool spot beneath a tree. They both sat in the shade and watched as the house crumbled into ash before their eyes.

Kid Palomino seemed distressed at the sight of the fire as it finished its vicious job. His eyes appeared strangely hollow, as if remembering another fire, at another place, in another time.

Red Rivers walked up to the pair, scratching his head. He handed his partner back the gunbelt. Palomino placed the guns on the ground between his legs.

'Did you know this lady was in there, Kid?' the older man questioned.

'I saw her through the window as we rode up.'

'Thank God.' The young woman coughed, trying to clear her throat of the taste of charcoal. 'I would have been a goner if you hadn't arrived when you did.'

Kid Palomino placed his filthy hand upon her shoulder and noticed the small holes that had been burnt into the fabric.

'You okay, Miss?' he asked, coughing.

'Thanks to you,' the female replied.

Kid Palomino drew in a deep breath and sighed. He was almost bone dry after only a few seconds in that fire, but he was sore from the licking heat.

His eyes surveyed her body for burns. She had a few, but as yet had not realized her injuries. It was clear to him that she required the attention of a good doctor to avoid being scarred for life.

'Is the town nearby, Miss?' he asked.

'About two miles down the trail,' she replied breathlessly.

'Get my hat, Red.' Palomino pointed at his Stetson which was near the trough.

Rivers walked across to the trough and watched the last of the flames consuming the remainder of the wooden structure, before retrieving his partner's Stetson off the ground.

As he turned to return to his friend and the young woman, he stopped in his tracks and noticed something on a nearby hill.

He moved close to the other two and kicked Palomino's boot gently as he indicated with his head. The Kid got to his feet and concentrated on what his partner was staring at.

A small party of Indians on ponies near the edge of the forest seemed to be watching what was occurring below. The feathers of their lances were clearly visible.

'You have any trouble with Indians, Miss?' the young man asked as he placed his hat on his head and stooped to pick up the gunbelt.

'Never had any trouble with them, Mister. Why?' she asked, as the man buckled up his belt and checked his two pistols.

Kid Palomino pointed the barrel of one of his guns at the hill before holstering it. She looked at the Indians with tired eyes before looking back at the two men.

'They never have given me any bother,' she wheezed.

'So it weren't them that set fire to your house?' Red asked thoughtfully.

'I guess it could have been but . . .'

Kid Palomino led her back behind the tree in the corner of her garden. Red followed.

'How did this fire start?'

'Beats me.' She shook her head.

Red watched as the Indians rode their ponies back into the trees. Then they were gone from view.

'Those are Utes, Kid.' Red rubbed the back of his neck as he spoke.

'Utes?' the Kid shrugged. 'You could tell their tribe from that distance?'

'Yep,' Red grinned. If there was one thing he knew about, it was Indians.

'They were Utes.' Palomino shrugged in acceptance of his partner's superior knowledge.

'You reckon this fire was deliberately set, Palomino?' Red asked his partner.

'Couldn't you smell it?' the Kid asked.

'Smell what, Palomino?'

'Coal-oil,' he answered. 'Coal-oil.'

Red sniffed the air and then nodded.

'Ya right. That is coal-oil all right.'

The young woman's face went white as she slumped forward into the young man's arms. Kid Palomino scooped her up into his strong arms and stood holding her unconscious body.

'Quick. Get the horses, Red,' Palomino coughed.

'Right, Kid. This girl needs a doctor real bad,' Red said as he ran toward the two mounts, which were standing nervously watching the smoking remains of the farmhouse.

Palomino gently handed the young girl to his partner as he quickly mounted. Then, stooping down from his saddle, he pulled her limp body up carefully in front of him. Red Rivers handed his partner the reins, which Palomino then used to steer his mount out from the yard onto the trail.

Rivers swung up into his saddle and cantered up beside his friend as they headed slowly toward Badwater Creek.

TWO

Standing on the porch of the doctor's house, Red and the Kid waited. They had been waiting for over an hour and it was starting to get dark. They had been waiting so long that Kid Palomino had traced his thumbnail around the doctor's shingle several dozen times, causing the paint to peel off. 'DOCTOR GERALD JENKINS', it read. The tree-lined streets were a welcome sight compared to the desert the two men had endured for ten days. The hotel opposite had lit all its lamps, and the saloon down the way was beginning to get noisy. The small white-washed church at the end of the long street seemed one of those quiet places that only came to life on Sunday mornings, remaining neglected for the remainder of the week. The large cast-iron bell could be easily seen up in the tower.

That's how it was in most towns these two drifters visited, but Badwater Creek might be the exception to the rule.

The door opened behind them as the doctor

16

stepped up to the two strangers.

'How is she, Doc?' Red Rivers asked, getting up from his perch on the white-painted fence that surrounded the porch.

The doctor stood thoughtfully, and Kid Palomino watched the elderly, silver-haired man closely.

'She's OK, considering her ordeal,' he answered.

'Will she be all right?' the Kid questioned.

'The burns have been tended,' the doctor said, 'but the smoke she inhaled will take a while to clear.'

'Me and Red are going over to the hotel. I'll cover your costs, Doctor.' Palomino patted the old man's arm.

'Considering what that young lady has gone through, I don't have the heart to charge any fee, son.'

Palomino stepped down from the porch and untied his horse from the rail. He wondered where this woman would live when she was well again.

'By the way,' he started, 'what's her name?'

'Lucy Hall,' the doctor replied. 'What shall I tell her if she asks what your name is, son?'

'They call me Palomino, and this is my partner, Red.'

'Kid Palomino?' the white-haired old man queried.

'Yep, Doc.'

'I'll tell her she was saved by two famous lawmen.'

The doctor went back inside the building as the two men reached the hotel.

Kid Palomino gave the reins of his horse to his friend and removed the saddle-bags from both mounts, before tossing them over his sore shoulder.

'Take Nugget down to the livery-stable with your nag whilst I get us a room for the night, Red.' The Kid stepped up onto the boardwalk as his friend led the two horses down the dark street toward the livery stable.

'My Derby ain't no nag, Palomino!' Red Rivers shouted over his shoulder. 'Maybe he ain't as pretty as Nugget, but he's a fine horse. That ain't no way to talk to a famous lawman.'

'Stop talking to yourself!' Palomino shouted after his pal.

All eyes were fixed upon the tall figure of Kid Palomino as he entered the hotel and crossed the carpeted floor, toward the desk where a balding man named Frank Giles stood with the open register before him.

Palomino was aware of his appearance and the burns on his clothing as he approached the small man.

'Yes, sir?' the little man asked.

'Got a room with a couple of nice feather-beds?' The Kid picked up the pen and dipped the nib into the inkwell. 'Me and my partner have had a rough ten days.'

'Yes, sir,' the man replied, watching the man fill in the register before resting his pen on the blotter. Swinging the book around he read the two names.

Kid Palomino.
Red Rivers.

His eyes looked up into the tall man's blue eyes, which seemed to shine from behind the black, smoke-marked features.

'Would you like for me to arrange a bath in your room, Mister Palomino?' he asked.

'That would be fine. Real fine, friend.'

The small balding man hit the desk bell a couple of times before a young teenage boy appeared from nowhere, panting, out of breath. Handing the key across to the boy, the man instructed the lad.

'Take this gentleman to Room 20 and get Walker to get a tub ready.'

'Yes, Mr Giles.' The boy looked at his boss, then at Palomino, and led the way to the stairs. The tall figure wearing the gunbelt moved up the thick carpet on the stairs behind the boy. The young boy had never seen a matching pair of pearl-handled Colt .45 Peacemakers in a hand-tooled gunbelt before. He kept turning to stare at the shooting rig. Halfway up, Palomino removed his hat and stared down at the gathering who were surrounding the registration desk to get a look at the names on the register. He continued up to the landing and trailed the young teenager along the corridor until they reached Room 20.

Palomino watched as the lad inserted the key into the lock and turned the key. The door opened smoothly, and the Kid gave a silver dollar to the boy as he accepted the key. The young man struck a match and lit the lamp next to the door. The room illuminated, and was quite decent. Two beds, a washstand, a fireplace and a wardrobe.

'I'll get Mr Walker to help me bring the tub.' The lad smiled, looking at the shining coin in the palm of his hand.

'Thank you . . .' Palomino said, in a way that compelled the young man to reveal his name.

'I'm Clark, sir.'

'I'm called Palomino, Clark.'

The tall man closed the door as the lad rushed away to find the character known as Walker, whoever he was. The thought of a soak in a tub of soapy warm water appealed to the injured Kid Palomino.

Pulling off his damaged shirt he could see it was beyond repair. A tall, full-length mirror on the wardrobe allowed him to study his burns. Palomino had been badly burned in over twenty spots across his arms and torso. His eyes studied the red, sore marks and the blistered skin. He could feel further burns on his back, but they were out of his line of sight. Only his black cowboy boots were still intact.

The door opened as Clark helped a strange grey-haired man with a long moustache carry the tin tub into the room. They placed it before the fireplace. The man who Palomino assumed was Walker left without saying a single word, whilst young Clark struck a match and put it to the already-prepared fire in the grate.

The blaze was welcome, and took the chill off the room quickly.

'I'll get the maid to bring the hot water, Palomino.'

'Fine.' The Kid smiled as the lad was leaving the room, preparing to close the door behind him. 'Has this town got a good clothes store?'

'Sure has,' Clark smiled.

Palomino sat on the edge of the bed after he had removed his gunbelt and hung it over the brass bed post. Bending down, he undid his spurs and tossed them onto the floor. Just then, the door opened and a young slim girl aged about nineteen entered, carrying a jug of hot water. She was very attractive, with long, brown hair. Her dark eyes had the longest eyelashes Palomino had ever seen. Their eyes met as she poured the contents of the jug into the tub. Her face showed no sign of interest in the stranger.

Kid Palomino sat watching as the girl turned silently and left the room. He smiled to himself as he managed to pull off his left boot and stocking. He tossed the sock away, as it smelled the way a sock always smells when it has been worn for ten solid days in the confines of a boot. He repeated the action with the right foot, and sat exercising his stiff toes.

The door opened once more, and this time it was Clark carrying another jug of hot water. He poured the steaming water into the tub, trying not to splash any over the carpet.

'Clark?'

'Yes, sir?'

'What's that girl's name?'

'Annie. Annie Brown,' came the reply, as the lad rushed out of the room.

For over twenty minutes the two youngsters took it in turns to bring hot water for the bathtub until it was half-full.

'Is that enough water, sir?' Annie Brown asked the sitting Kid Palomino.

He nodded, smiling.

'That's fine, Annie,' he said.

For a moment she paused, as if stunned this man knew her name. He stood and strolled across the carpet toward her. She appeared very nervous as he held out a hand with a silver dollar.

'No thank you,' she said, refusing the tip. 'How do you know my name?'

'I asked Clark,' Palomino replied.

'Why do that?' She looked confused by his interest.

'No reason, I guess,' he shrugged.

Her stunning looks seemed wasted in this dead-end job, but she seemed perfectly satisfied with her lot.

Without saying anything else she left the room, closing the door behind her. The Kid flipped the coin in the air and caught it before returning it to his pants pocket.

He unbuckled his belt and slid it out of the belt-loops of his pants before tossing it upon the bed. He moved to the saddle-bags, and tossed his partner's over onto the other bed. Opening his bags, he pulled out a fresh shirt and a pair of pants. They were pale blue, the same as the outfit he had ruined during his act of savng Lucy Hall's life.

Resting the fresh clothes over the brass rail of his bed, he heard the door open behind him once more.

Upon turning, he watched as Red Rivers staggered in like a man who had very sore feet. Every step brought another strained expression upon the red-bearded face.

Red looked down at the bathtub as he tossed his hat across the room. As he walked he discarded items of clothing. Each item landed on the floor, sending dust clouds up. When he got to his pink long johns he flopped onto the soft bed and gave a satisfied sigh of relief.

'You ought to have a bath after me, Red,' Palomino said, taking off his pants and long under-pants and stepping cautiously into the tub. The water was still quite hot as he gently tried to ease himself into the liquid. After several bounces on the water he finally submerged his rear into it and sat blowing out, trying to cope with the incredible sensation.

'Nah, you can wash, I'll just sleep,' Red Rivers yawned, as he lay watching his partner who was start-ing to look like a lobster in the tin tub. Then Red's tired eyes saw the door open once more, and the young beauty named Annie Brown enter.

Without hesitating Annie walked up to the tub and

stared down at Kid Palomino. He jumped in shock as he looked up into her emotionless face.

She dropped a large block of soap into the water between his legs.

'Soap,' she said, staring down as the man tried to cover his modesty. 'OK?'

'Uh . . . uh . . . OK,' Palomino stuttered.

The water had splashed into his eyes as the bar of soap landed into the bath. He gazed up at her face as she paused for a moment staring down into the clear water. Her face did not flicker with interest of any sort, it remained stony yet still beautiful. The naked man in the water might as well have been a potted plant.

Then she looked up and stared at Red Rivers, before turning silently and walking out of the room.

Palomino seemed to look at the closed door for several moments before he turned to his partner who was smiling on his bed.

'Did you see that?' Palomino gasped in total disbelief.

'Yep,' Red chuckled. 'You sure impressed her, Kid.'

Three

'You have no imagination,' Kid Palomino said, looking at his partner as he watched the morning sunshine through the window drapes.

'Curiosity killed the cat, Kid.'

'Then we better be very careful,' Palomino smiled.

'If we saddled up and lit out of this town, we wouldn't have to be careful,' Red grinned.

Red crawled out from his bed, dragged himself over to the window and stood scratching himself as he stared down into the street, yawning.

'What time is it again, Kid?' he asked feebly.

Palomino leaned against the wall looking at the sight of his partner in the well-worn long johns.

'Get dressed, Red.'

'What's the hurry?' Rivers ambled to his clothes and started to pull his legs into the baggy pants.

'You look bad when you're dressed, but in your long underwear you are a sight to behold, Red.'

Red Rivers looked up through the strands of his uncombed hair at his friend.

He managed to dress and followed his friend out of the room. Palomino locked the room door and led the way down the tall stairs toward the lobby. Although his partner carried his Stetson in his hand, Rivers decided to wear his battered headwear.

A few people who were seated around the wide lobby looked up from their newspapers and stared at the pair as they descended.

Palomino walked up to the man behind the counter and handed the key to him. This man was sleepy, very sleepy.

'We like the room,' Kid Palomino stated. 'We are staying for a few more days.'

'Fine,' the man answered, trying to focus on the pair.

'Don't let our room,' Red sniffed at the man, ''coz we'll be back.'

'Wonderful.' The man hung the key on the hook behind him under the number '20'. 'I can hardly contain my glee.'

'Nice fella,' Red smiled to his tall friend. Kid Palomino lifted the hat and placed it carefully onto his head as they turned.

Red ambulated behind his partner as they left the hotel and walked out onto the boardwalk.

'Where we going?'

'For a ride,' Palomino replied.

Four

The morning air was chilled by the breeze that drifted from the far-away mountains. This sunshine was deceptive. Its clean, pure light had no heat in it. The two riders gritted their teeth as they steered their mounts toward the remains of Lucy Hall's house.

The ashes were being blown across the fields as they arrived, yet the bulk of charred wood remained where it had fallen. The shape of the building made a curious black imprint upon the surrounding area. It was as if the soil had been branded by a giant rustler.

It was a sad sight.

The Kid slowly pulled up on his reins as he approached the hitching-rail that stood alone outside the white picket fence.

'What the heck we come back here for, Kid?' Red said, steadying his horse.

Palomino smiled at his friend as he dismounted.

'To look around.' The Kid tossed his reins over the rail and tied it securely, and Rivers copied his actions.

'What we looking for?' Red asked, as they went through the open gateway and paced toward the remains of what was once a well-cared-for home.

'Clues.' Palomino shivered as the breeze cut through his clothing.

'Not clues.' Red shook his head. He hated it when his pal was looking for clues. Mainly because he had no idea what clues were. All he knew was that clues equalled trouble.

'Yep. Clues.' Palomino walked around the black outline of the ruins. It was a forlorn sight. To see traces of someone's entire life reduced to this black mess was chilling to both men.

Red Rivers followed his partner looking around at the black area.

'We are gonna get ourselves into trouble again,' he muttered under his breath. 'Clues is trouble.'

'Probably,' Palomino smiled. He stared carefully at the ground as he slowly walked.

'Why we sticking our noses into this, Kid?' Red gave a sigh as he spoke. 'We have business in Wyoming.'

'I know about our business in Wyoming, Red.'

'Then what we hanging around in Colorado for?'

Kid Palomino kneeled down and brushed at the ashes with his fingers.

'We got nothing better to do.'

Red shivered as he stood beside his pal.

'We have a job waiting for us up in—'

'Look at this, Red.' Palomino pointed at his discovery.

Rivers leaned forward and focused.

'What is it?'

'Silver,' Palomino answered. He picked up the small fragment in his fingers, before rising slowly to his feet. His eyes stared at the object in the palm of his hand. There was a knowledgeable expression on his face. This small piece of silver told a story that he was able to read.

'So it's silver,' Red shrugged. 'It's probably a melted ring belonging to the Hall woman.'

Palomino shook his head in disagreement with his friend.

'This is raw silver, Red,' he said quietly.

'What ya mean by raw silver?' The older man squinted at the object.

'This is silver that was in the soil. It got heated up due to the blaze.' The Kid handed the small piece of metal to Rivers and knelt down once more, picking up another, then another.

'I still don't get it,' Rivers said thoughtfully. 'Silver is silver, ain't it?'

'Nope.' The tall figure stood next to him and dropped more particles into his partner's hands. 'Silver is sort of blue sludge in its natural state. It's only when it's refined or heated up to a great temperature that it turns into the shiny stuff we use for rings and suchlike.'

'Blue sludge?' Red Rivers rubbed the metal in his hands vigorously and gasped as it started to glint.

'Yep. Blue sludge.' The Kid wandered away from the house and started to use the heel of his boot to dig at the ground. Then he scooped up a handful of dirt and turned to his partner.

Rivers' jaw fell when he saw the blue sludge in his friend's palm.

'Is that muck . . . silver?' he asked.

'Pure silver, buddy.' Palomino brushed his hands together and wiped the valuable find onto the ground.

'How you know so much about silver?'

'I knew a man who dug for gold once,' the Kid began. 'All he kept finding was this blue sludge. Messy stuff. He tossed it all to one side and kept digging. No gold, just this blue muck. He gave up his claim and left the site. Then somebody from back east came across the blue sludge mountain the man had discarded. He knew it was pure silver, and made a fortune.'

'Who was the dumb guy who dumped a fortune of silver?'

'My brother,' Palomino smiled.

Rivers had no idea his partner even had a brother up until that moment.

'What your brother do?'

'He became a drunkard.'

'Can't blame him, I guess.' Red followed the tall

man around the shape of the building that was etched into the ground.

'Getting your brain pickled because you made a mistake is a waste, Red,' Palomino said as he pointed at the bushes where two empty coal-oil cans lay. 'There they are.'

Red walked up to the cans and kicked them.

'Why would anyone want to burn this lady out?'

'To get their hands on a chunk of land with silver three inches under the top soil, Red.'

'That seems a good reason, Kid.'

'Come on.' The Kid strode toward their waiting horses with his friend in hasty pursuit.

'Where we off to now?' Red puffed as he put the chunks of silver into his vest pocket.

'To town.' Palomino untied his reins from the pole and gathered them up, before holding onto the saddle-horn and putting his left foot into the stirrup.

Red watched as his pal swung his leg over the saddle and seated himself firmly.

'To town?' He mounted quickly and pulled the reins up to force his horse to turn away from the hitching-rail. 'What in blazes for?'

Kid Palomino's eyes narrowed as he spurred his horse.

'To eat. I'm hungry.'

Red Rivers had to slap the neck of his faithful horse 'Derby' in order to catch up with his galloping friend. As he raced up beside the palomino stallion he looked across at his young partner's face. As usual, he had no idea what was going on inside the man's mind.

If Kid Palomino had one fault, it was his lack of selfishness – his willingness to risk everything for a total stranger.

Rivers rode alongside the brooding, thinking rider. He knew from experience it was better to let the man think when he was in this mood. And if anyone could think . . . it was the Kid.

The pair had only been riding for a few minutes when, through the thick tree line to their left, they saw it.

Smoke.

'Not again?' Red shook his head as they pulled their mounts to a halt.

Palomino stood in his stirrups as he stared hard at the trees until he was certain of the fire's direction.

'Follow me, Red,' the Kid said as he slapped the loose reins hard across Nugget's flank. The horse took off like a puma from a tree and started up the steep rise toward a cutting between the tall trees.

Rivers spurred his horse and followed his friend.

The men found themselves in the darkness of the wood on a narrow trail that twisted its way through the tall, thin pines. The sun had trouble penetrating through the dense canopy of branches overhead. The trail was so narrow that they had to ride single file as they galloped. Red sat flat in his saddle and held on for dear life as his faithful Derby tracked the man on the palomino stallion ahead.

The Kid somehow was able to ride whilst standing in his stirrups and lean so far over his saddle-horn that his head seemed to be brushing Nugget's mane.

Onward and upward they chased.

The smell of the smoke now filled their nostrils as they approached the clearing on top of the hillside. In the clearing a house blazed furiously. Smoke swirled around in the wind and red embers floated in all directions.

Palomino seemed to jump from the horse as they got close to the dwelling, then stopped as the heat forced him back.

This time they were too late.

Too late to do anything.

Anything except watch.

They watched the fire consume the building as if it were made of tissue paper. The walls caved in, and soon all that remained were the rough stone chimney, and a few timber uprights.

Rivers stayed in his saddle and held onto his friend's horse's bridle as he watched the Kid.

The tall figure seemed transfixed upon the scene. He stood shielding his face from the heat with his hand and unable to move away.

'Kid?' Red called over at his younger pal above the noise of crackling wood. 'Kid?'

Finally, the young man turned and walked toward his partner. It might have been the smoke-filled air but, for Red Rivers, it was a sight he had never seen before. There were stains down Palomino's cheeks. Stains of tears.

'You okay, Kid?' Red asked, concerned by his friend's reaction to the fire.

Palomino grabbed the reins and mounted Nugget.

'Yeah.'

'You seem upset.' Rivers put his hand across onto the young man's shoulders. 'What's wrong?'

'I don't like fires,' Palomino replied quietly.

'Why, Kid?'

'As long as you live,' the Kid glared at the still-raging inferno, 'never ask me that question again.'

'OK.' Red Rivers knew something was deadly wrong with his friend. Whatever the reason, he knew it was better never to ask.

'Smell it?' Palomino sniffed at the smoke.

'Coal-oil?'

'Yeah. Coal-oil, again.' Palomino was about to pull his mount away from the clearing and retrace their route when a shot rang out and sent a chunk off a nearby pine tree splattering into his face.

Then several more shots followed, and the two men found themselves in the middle of a shooting gallery where they were the targets. Both horses reared up in reaction to the bullets that were speeding past them.

Palomino pulled his Winchester from the saddle-sheath, before throwing himself from the mount and rolling across the ground until he found cover behind a large boulder. He cranked the carbine into action and started to return the fire quickly, as he watched Red dismounting and rush into a thicket of trees.

The red-haired man held his pistol at arm's length and fired from his position beside a tall wide tree. Each shot from his hand-gun was matched by two from his partner's rifle.

Their only target was the gunsmoke that hung in mid-air in the darkness of the tree line opposite. The house still blazed, and a black shroud swirled down over the scene every few seconds as the wind changed. It was clear that there were three gunmen firing at the pair, from the miniature smoke signals in the dark wood behind the clearing.

A bullet passed by Palomino's cheek. He could feel the heat of the lead and ducked. Another volley of firing seemed to rip up the tree beside Red Rivers, causing him to fall to his knees covered in tree bark. He furiously wiped his beard to remove the fresh, warm sawdust. It smelled of charcoal, and for a moment the ginger-whiskered man thought his prized growth was alight.

Noticing his partner was under heavy fire, the Kid quickly tossed down his empty carbine, drew both his .45s and started to send lead in the direction of their attackers. The matched Peacemakers fired in unison from his steady hands.

Red loaded his pistol once more from his gunbelt and started to join in on the firing. The tree that he had chosen was again being hit by numerous bullets, sending splinters flying above his head. He pulled his hat down over his ears and continued firing. Bullet after bullet was met with an equal return of deadly intent from the men they had yet to see.

Palomino crawled through the long grass to use the still-raging fire as cover. He lay on his back as he quickly emptied the spent cartridges from his guns before reloading them.

He was about to start firing again when a remaining burnt timber from the house fell in his direction, causing him to roll down into a ditch. The smouldering wooden joist bounced where only seconds earlier the Kid had been lying.

The exchange had lasted for several minutes before Palomino and Rivers noticed that their two horses had deserted the scene for safer ground down the trail.

Then, as quickly as it had started, the firing ceased. Perhaps their attackers were low on shells, Red thought.

The Kid could hear horses beyond the burning house and men making noises as they were desperately making their escape.

He got to his feet and fired both his Colts into the blackness of the dense trees. He heard a faint, distant cry.

'I winged one of them!' he called to his partner, as Red came up to his side.

'You sure?' Rivers asked, looking around for more trouble.

'I hit one of them,' Palomino snapped.

'You winged one. Yep, you did.' Red patted his friend on the shoulder and then scratched his head. 'Any idea where our horses are, Kid?'

'They lit out.' The Kid was angry. 'Damn, I could have caught up with them bushwhackers—'

'Not on foot.' Red holstered his gun and started to head back down the trail they had earlier ridden up.

Palomino started to follow.

'Red?'

The older man paused for an instant.

'What, Palomino?'

'Sorry.'

Red Rivers grinned, grabbed the man's arm and started down the trail in search for their two mounts.

'I reckon this is a nice day for a stroll, what about you?'

'Could be warmer.'

'Warmer? I'm sweating like a Georgia hog now, Kid.'

'So am I, come to think about it.' The young man smiled again as they made their way carefully down the dark, steep trail. Then they saw the two horses waiting for them about fifty feet ahead. These animals were no strangers to gun-play, and knew when they heard bullets starting to fly it was safer to get out of the way, fast. Real fast.

Riding away from the new fire, through the tall trees back down onto the trail that led toward

Badwater Creek, the two men dwelt upon the recent incidents.

Whoever it was that had set the latest fire was probably the same bunch that had burned Lucy Hall out.

They knew why.

All they needed to know was who.

Who?

The ride back toward Badwater Creek was a long, silent one as both men thought hard. Red Rivers trotted his horse alongside his partner and watched his friend. Never had he seen this normally cool man so worked up. Exactly why the tall man was so upset by these fires, Red could only guess.

They drifted back into the town and allowed their mounts to walk quietly down the centre of the main street. It was busier now than it had been when they had set out. A stagecoach stood outside the Wells Fargo depot as the townsfolk scurried back and forth. Even with all the activity in Badwater Creek, it was still very early.

'What time is it?' Red asked, sitting in his saddle.

'Breakfast time, according to my belly, Red,' the Kid responded, as he turned his mount up to the hitching-rail outside the doctor's house.

Palomino slid off his saddle and handed the reins to his partner.

The Kid stepped up onto the boardwalk and used his knuckles to knock on the door. He waited for a few moments before the door was answered by the old medical man.

'Kid,' the doc greeted him with a tired smile.

'How's the patient?' The Kid looked down into the man's eyes with a concern that the old man had rarely seen in recent times.

'Still resting.'

'She gonna be OK?' There was consideration in his voice.

'I think so.' The old man gave the young, tall man a knowing glance. 'If you call back at about six tonight I think she'll be well enough to see you.'

'OK.' Palomino nodded, and withdrew to his mount.

'You boys going out for a ride?'

'Coming back,' Rivers corrected, as his partner mounted beside him.

The three men exchanged nods and the two riders carried on back down the long street, as the doctor went back inside his home.

'Where we gonna eat?' Red asked, as they weaved their steeds between the various obstacles in the street. 'I fancy a thick steak with onions.'

Palomino looked straight ahead at the saloon.

'We could try in there.'

'Not a steakhouse?' Red Rivers queried. 'I could be wrong here, Kid, but I always thought that when you wanted to eat you went to places that sold grub and if you were thirsty you went to a saloon. Well?'

'I want a beer.' Palomino glanced at his friend.

'You drink a beer in the morning?'

'Why not?' Palomino headed Nugget to a vacant hitching-rail and pointed to three horses standing at another rail. Three tired horses that were lathered up after a long, hard ride. Three horses that were steaming.

'Come to think of it, I could use a beer too.' Red dismounted, tied his horse to the rail and then walked past the three mounts, running his hand along the neck of one. The heavy sweat on his fingers smelled bad. He swished his hand in the trough before stepping up onto the boardwalk next to the waiting Kid.

'Notice the mare's saddle?' Palomino said quietly.

'Yep. There's a lot of blood on that saddle.'

'I told you that I winged one of them.' Palomino headed toward the saloon swing-doors and entered with Rivers on his tail. There were droplets of blood leading from the horse tied up at the hitching-rail right up to the saloon's doors. Inside the saloon was a different matter. The floor inside was covered in a thick layer of fresh sawdust. Any drops of blood here had been absorbed by the porous sawdust. Red stayed close to Palomino as they entered, it was a routine they had gone through so many times that it was now second nature.

Red Rivers knew how to cover his partner's back, and his eyes were everywhere as they walked up to the bar. He knew that Kid Palomino was direct and often to the point.

He would take a course of action and often

become unaware that his mark had friends with guns. Rivers would watch everyone, and could spot a back-shooter at a hundred feet. How many times had his eagle eyes saved the younger man's life during their days as peace officers? Probably the same amount of times that Palomino's speedy draw and accuracy had saved his.

The bar was quiet.

Too quiet.

Apart from the bartender, they were alone. The bartender was a large man with a waxed moustache and a belly that had enjoyed many glasses of beer. He looked shady. The Kid noticed the bead of perspiration trickling down into his stiff collar as they approached him. The emptiness of the bar was a strange sight.

That made both men nervous. The three horses outside were exhausted and their riders had entered this saloon, yet they were not in the bar.

Palomino's eyes glanced around the area and, apart from the tall staircase which led to a myriad of rooms, there were also two other doors on the ground floor.

Rivers leaned against his partner and spoke out of the corner of his mouth through the red whiskers.

'The blood seems to have been soaked up by the sawdust, Kid.'

'Yeah,' Kid replied. 'But it led in here.'

Red turned and smiled at the bartender licking his dry lips.

41

'What will it be, boys?' the bartender asked nervously.

Palomino's eyes narrowed.

'Two beers and three bushwhackers.'

'One bushwhacker with a hole in him,' Red added.

'I don't understand, boys.' The man started to pull two beers. 'What you mean by bushwhackers?'

'Who came in here before us?' Palomino questioned.

'You are my first customers this morning, gents.'

Kid Palomino glared at the man who pushed the two glasses in front of them. Red Rivers lifted the glass to his whiskers and swallowed some suds, as his partner lifted his glass and studied the rising bubbles.

'I'll ask you one more time,' the Kid said quietly. 'Who came into this bar before we did?'

'Nobody.' The barman was sweating heavily now.

Palomino tossed the beer in the man's face, before placing the glass back onto the bartop. He tossed a coin onto the wet wooden surface, then grabbed the man by his shirt and pulled him toward him. The terrified, wet man stared into the burning eyes of Kid Palomino.

Then the swing-doors made a noise behind them, and Red tapped his partner's side. Palomino released the bartender and turned to stare at the man with the star on his vest who was walking toward them.

'What you boys doing to Charlie?'

'Nothing much, Sheriff,' Rivers replied quickly to the man who wore the star and a fancy shooting-rig.

'I'm Bob Davis, Sheriff of Badwater Creek.' The man was about forty and looked experienced. The single gun hung low on his hip as he moved in on the pair. 'You two troublemakers?'

'Nope,' Palomino answered, as the man stepped before him. He was tall, but not as tall as the Kid.

'Throwing beer over a bartender seems like trouble to me, boys,' Davis noted.

'It was just a way of getting him to remember something, Sheriff,' Red Rivers shrugged as he finished his beer.

'I don't cotton to that sort of thing,' Davis snarled at them, resting his hand on the hammer of his gun.

'We had good reason to be angry,' Palomino informed the man.

'What reason?'

'Earlier we discovered a blazing house up in the woods near Lucy Hall's place—' the Kid started.

'That's Old Man Smith's house,' Sheriff Davis nodded.

'It was burned out by a few guys who opened up on us when we rode in on the scene,' Rivers continued.

'I heard one of the men cry out when I fired at them.'

'You see them?' Davis asked.

'Nope.' Palomino shook his head. 'But when we

43

got back to town we saw three horses tied up outside here, and one had blood on the saddle. The blood led in here.'

'That is pretty damn thin.' Davis moved around the pair. 'I bet you never thought that perhaps a ranch hand might have cut his hand on some barb-wire?'

'What?' Kid Palomino raised a doubtful eyebrow.

'You see a horse with blood on the saddle and suddenly it has to belong to the man you plugged up at Smith's place?' Davis rested his elbows on the bar and watched the two men. 'You ain't got no proof of what you suspect, have you?'

'I guess not,' Palomino admitted.

'This bartender here said nobody came in here before us but the blood drops come right up to the front door, Sheriff Davis,' Red said, exasperated.

Davis looked at Charlie the bartender.

'Did anyone come in here before these hotheads, Charlie?'

'No, Sheriff,' Charlie replied.

'Guess that's that, boys,' Sheriff Davis shrugged. 'I suggest you quit while you're ahead.'

Kid Palomino nodded and stared down at the floor. He moved away from the bar with Rivers in close pursuit.

'We free to go?' the Kid asked the lawman.

'Yep.' Davis waved them away.

The two men walked to the swing-doors and pushed their way out into the street.

'What gives, Kid?' Red asked his pal.

'I have no idea, Red.' Palomino untied his horse and mounted then waited for his friend to copy his behaviour. 'But I reckon it's strange that Sheriff Davis didn't seem concerned that Old Man Smith's place had been burned to the ground.'

Red nodded in agreement as he spurred his horse into following Palomino toward the nearest steak-house.

Five

Kid Palomino stood beside his seated partner Red Rivers, sipping coffee, staring out of the large window of the steakhouse. Directly outside their two mounts stood almost motionless against the hitching rail. Neither mount obstructed the view though. Both men had eaten their meals and now were on their fourth coffee each. Palomino kept watching the trio of horses outside the saloon with an almost fanatical concentration.

'What are we still doing in here, Palomino?' Rivers enquired from his seat beside the table with its chequered cloth. 'I'm getting bored.'

'Get yourself some more pie,' the Kid said into his cup.

'Sounds good, but what the heck are we doing here?'

'Eating, Red.'

'We quit eating a while ago,' Red smiled, putting his thumbs into his pants and trying to get some leverage.

'The horses are still outside the saloon,' Palomino noted, as he lowered the empty cup onto the table top.

'So what the heck does that mean?' Red got to his feet, and suddenly felt much heavier than when they had first arrived in town.

'I was wondering who would leave three lathered-up horses out in this wind for over an hour.' The Kid ran his fingers through his hair and blew out a sigh of frustration at the window pane.

'Folks who couldn't give a damn about their horses.' Rivers put his foot on the hard chair next to his friend.

Palomino then tapped his partner's leg and pointed out toward the saloon. A man was gathering up the reins of the three horses and starting to lead them down the street toward them. They watched as the man rounded the corner, pulling the tired mounts behind him.

'Who do you reckon that is, Red?'

Red Rivers pressed his face against the glass of the window and squinted at the man.

'That's the guy from the livery-stable,' he said knowingly.

'Yeah?' Kid Palomino picked up his hat from off the edge of the table and placed it onto his head. 'Come on.'

Rivers tossed a couple of dollars onto the table and tipped his hat to the waitress, then he scurried behind the tall man who had walked out into the cold street.

The wind was starting to get vicious as it tore through the streets of Badwater Creek. The few trees that occasioned themselves around the town were losing leaves as the wind ripped through them. The sun was still as bright, but now was even less effective than before.

The two men paced along the boardwalks after the man who was leading the three horses toward his stables. He had placed all three in separate stalls when the two men entered the livery.

'Howdy, Mr Rivers,' Fred Jones, the livery-stable owner, greeted the red-haired man, as he approached with the tall man at his side. 'Who's your friend?'

'Hi, Fred,' Red nodded. 'This is my partner. They call him Kid Palomino.'

'Palomino? I heard of you. You is a lawman.' Fred busied himself with removing the first horse's saddle and starting to rub the steed down.

'Why did you go and get these horses from outside the saloon, Fred?' Palomino questioned the simple man.

Fred straightened up and looked at the two men with a curious expression upon his face.

'They was sweating up and it's getting windy.'

'Yeah, but why did you go and get them?'

'I couldn't leave them in that state.'

'So you just brought them here to tend to them?' Red interrupted.

'Nope. The sheriff told me to get them.' Fred

grinned, showing his large teeth. So many large teeth for one small head.

'Sheriff Davis told you to get the horses?'

'Yep,' Jones nodded.

'Whose horses are they?'

'They belong to the Lady G Saloon,' Fred grinned.

'Who owns the Lady G Saloon?' Palomino rubbed his chin thoughtfully.

The stable-owner seemed to be thinking. 'Matt Davis,' he replied with another nod.

'Another Davis?' Rivers gave his partner a glance.

'Yep, the sheriff's older brother.' Fred rubbed the cloth along the steaming horse gently but firmly. 'He owns another few places around town.'

'What sort of places does Matt Davis own, Fred?' Palomino rested his arms on a wooden partition. His eyes were glued to this odd man.

'There is another saloon down the far end of town.' Fred blushed. 'Ain't very good beer but it has ladies there.'

'Ladies?' The Kid raised an eyebrow and a smile crossed his face. 'What you mean by ladies, Fred?'

'You know. Soiled doves.' Jones winked.

'Oh.' Red perked up.

'What else does Matt Davis own?' the Kid enquired.

'Lots of things. I can't recall everything he got,' Fred grinned. 'He got a mine up in the hills someplace and—'

'A mine?' Red started to nod even more than Jones.

'Yep. A gold-mine.'

'Did you say gold?' Palomino stood upright. 'You sure it's a gold-mine?'

'Sure am. I worked there for a while a few years ago, before my Uncle Silas died and left me this business.' Fred Jones looked at his battered, weather-beaten livery-stable with pride. To him it was a palace. 'Now I is independent and I got money in the bank, to boot.'

Kid Palomino touched the brim of his Stetson and turned to leave, with Red on his heels.

'Where exactly is this gold-mine?' Red stopped to ask.

'About a quarter-mile east of the main trail, and up the big hill past Smith's place,' Fred answered automatically as he worked on the horses.

'How far up the trail past Smith's place?' Red quizzed.

'Right up near the top of the hill,' Fred added. 'Right through the trees and up along the clearing. There's a rock-face up there. Huge thing. You have to work your way around, but you gotta be careful.'

'How come?' The Kid moved around the livery, rubbing his chin in thought.

'They say there are mountain men up there and Indians and bears and lions and—' Fred would have carried on with his list of dangers to avoid around the big hill and the gold-mine if Palomino had allowed him. The Kid did not allow him to continue.

'Thanks, Fred!' the Kid shouted over his shoulder

and the noisy wind that was sweeping in through the large doors.

The two men walked away from the tall wooden structure, and headed back toward the steakhouse where their horses were tied up to the hitching-pole outside.

'What you thinking about, Kid?'

'Seems to be a lot of folks named Davis around here, Red.' The tall man smiled.

'We still ain't got no proof of nothing.' Rivers got to Derby first, and untied the horse before mounting.

Kid Palomino leaned on his saddle, holding onto the horn for a while, before stepping into the stirrup and swinging his leg over Nugget's broad back. He allowed the horse to step backward before turning the mount to face his friend.

'Let's go for a ride.'

'Where we going this time, Kid?'

The eyes of the taller rider narrowed once more.

'We might just have a quiet ride around the countryside, or we might just try and find out a few things.'

'What sort of things?'

'Like if there's silver on Old Man Smith's property, Red,' the Kid began, 'and if there's gold in that mine.'

The two riders spurred their mounts and raced down the long main street of Badwater Creek. As they passed the hotel the distinctive figure of Sheriff

Bob Davis stood watching their departure from town. He entered the lobby as the wall-clock struck noon, and approached the frail man behind the counter.

'Frank?'

'Yes, Sheriff?'

'Who are those two men who just rode off out of town?'

Frank Giles turned the register around and pointed at the two names.

'Kid Palomino and Red Rivers,' Davis read aloud. 'They were lawmen a while back, weren't they?'

'Still are, I reckon.'

Bob Davis grinned. It was not a grin of happiness. It was more a grin of fear.

Even Davis had heard about Kid Palomino and his partner. What he had heard made him concerned.

Very concerned.

Six

There had been silver on Old Man Smith's property all right just as there had been silver on Lucy Hall's.

Smith's property yielded one thing extra. A burned body in the heart of the ashes that had once been a house. The two men assumed this was Old Man Smith himself. They left the body where it lay, in case Sheriff Davis happened to ride out there to investigate the fire. Somehow, both Rivers and Palomino doubted that would happen.

Now they were riding through the thick trees until they found the trail, which could have been used by the three gunmen. The narrow, muddy trail was covered in horseshoe tracks. The Kid and his partner decided that this was a trail worth following.

As usual the big palomino stallion led the brown quarter-horse through the dense forest. They rode, being lashed by tree branches, for over a mile, when the trail forked.

Kid Palomino pulled Nugget to an abrupt halt. Red reined up hard to stop next to the tall figure.

'What you stop for?' Red asked as he gathered in his loose reins.

The Kid pointed at the fork in the trail.

'Which way?'

Rivers scratched his whiskers and gave the question a great deal of consideration.

'I figure the trail to the left heads uphill.'

'That seems logical.' His partner grinned, picking up his canteen and unscrewing the top.

Palomino drank the cool water from his canteen before handing it to his partner.

'You're right. We go to the left.'

'We do?' Red choked on the water as he handed the canteen back to palomino. 'You think I'm right?'

'Sure.' The Kid screwed the top back on the canteen and hung it back over the saddle-horn. 'Don't you?'

'Well, I weren't sure.' Red admitted, as he spurred Derby into following the large stallion up the trail which led to the left.

The two men rode for thirty minutes. Thirty minutes of uphill riding. Thirty minutes of being hit by thin branches that seemed to be everywhere.

There was one thing for certain. This trail had not been used for a very long time. The overgrown track was testament to that fact.

Then they reached the clearing.

The sun was overhead, and suddenly seemed blinding to the two riders who pulled their mounts up. Their eyes had become used to the darkness of the forest. Now they were forced to sit in their saddles and wait until they regained their vision. Palomino was first to get his sight back and used his sleeve to wipe away the sweat from his brow.

The clearing was vast. This must have been the highest point on this mountain. Ahead there were rocks that rose from the grass like a very tall wall. This was no man-made wall, however. This was a cliff-face carved by nature and designed for wild animals to enjoy. This was not a place any normal man might choose to visit by choice. This was a place you found by accident.

It grew as the two riders edged their horses closer to it. It was grey-and-white stone. A few patches of moss here and there but mostly just solid rock. If this was just a big hill and not a mountain, then the two riders never wanted to find a real mountain on their travels.

Palomino leaned against the castle of his saddle and tried to see the top of the cliff above their heads. It was a long way up to the top. An awfully long way.

They allowed the two horses to walk slowly along-side the grey wall of the cliff. Below them the trees seemed to fall away. Beyond the trees they could see forever. In the distance they could even see part of the Colordo River as it snaked its way through the scenery. This was a view that once witnessed, would be impossible to forget.

Then a shot rang out. It was over their heads, but both Palomino and Rivers knew it was time to dismount and use the long grass for cover.

It was certain that it had been a warning shot. Anyone worth their salt could have taken either of them off their mounts if they had wanted. Whoever had fired the shot had not wanted to shoot them. Just let them know they were not welcome.

The two men lay outstretched, holding their guns before them, watching ahead. They had cocked their guns, waiting for a target to show itself, but none came. No further shots came either.

'What gives?' Red whispered out of the corner of his mouth.

Palomino lay silently listening. He heard nothing for a while, then he could hear footsteps coming toward them through the tall grass. Footsteps that were so indistinct that he could not make out exactly where their adversary was.

'What's that?' Red asked.

The cranking of a Winchester about six feet before them sent the blood running through their veins as they cautiously lifted up their heads to look at whoever it was who had them dead to rights.

To the utter amazement of both Palomino and Rivers they were staring up at a young girl about sixteen or so. She held the rifle firmly, weaving it back and forth between her two targets.

'Get up, you claim-jumping varmints,' she growled in a voice that seemed to mean business.

'Easy, girl,' Red stuttered, as he raised his arms above his head. 'Don't shoot.'

'Drop them shooting-irons.' She ordered. 'Drop them now, or you is both dead meat.'

The two men did as they were told, dropping the guns into the soft, green grass. They both got carefully to their feet and held their arms up above their heads.

'You scum-sucking wasters.' She cursed as she looked up at them from behind her rust-covered rifle. 'Thought you could sneak up here on my blind side, did you?'

'We ain't no claim-jumpers, Missy,' Red blurted. 'Say something to the girl, Kid. I'm getting nervous.'

Her face was pretty, if a trifle dirty. Her hair was tied in two bunches and her jeans went right up under her chin. A home-made strap held the baggy pants up. Her footwear was home-made out of raw leather. She was a sight that neither man had ever seen before.

'You live up here?' Palomino smiled down at her.

'You are pretty for a man, ain't you?' she sneered.

Palomino gave a loud belly-laugh. He had been called hundreds of things by hundreds of people in his time, but he had never before been referred to as pretty.

'You are a tough one, Miss.' He smiled.

'I could whoop you.' She aimed the rifle at his head.

'I reckon you could at that,' Palomino agreed. Nobody had ever managed to get the drop on either him or Red before, yet this small female had done it.

57

She had somehow crept up on them without their being able to prevent it.

This was no ordinary young girl.

She moved around her two captives and forced them to walk ahead of her. They made no objections, and trod through the tall grass. She had picked up their guns and stuffed them down into her jeans. As they walked they began to see a smoking camp-fire ahead. A large fur skin hung out on a frame drying. It was the skin of a grizzly bear. An old tarpaulin was carefully strung up against the rock face and held out on two strong wooden stakes to create a practical shelter. They arrived at the camp and she moved in front of them.

'Sit.' She pointed at the ground next to the fire. They took the hint and sat down. It was warmer here. They were in the shelter of the rock-face and sitting on furs. The fire had a coffee-pot on it.

'Can I lower my arms and have a cup of coffee, please?' Kid Palomino asked the young female.

She was thoughtful.

'Who are you?' she asked.

'They call me Palomino and this is Red.' The Kid smiled as he lowered his arms carefully.

She sat across the fire from them and pulled a fur over her shoulders. The rifle, still aimed in the two men's direction, gave her total control over her captives.

'You one of them Davis boys?' she asked the Kid.

'Nope,' he answered honestly.

'You sure are pretty for a man, Mister.' She repeated her statement. It was not meant as a compliment but as a curious question. 'Why you named after your horse?'

'You're pretty yourself, Miss.' Palomino smiled, warming his hands at the fire. 'What they call you?'

'Nobody calls me anything,' she said. 'Not any more.'

'You alone up here?' Red mused.

'Now.' She looked sad for a split second, before her expression reverted back.

'What's your name?' the Kid asked softly.

It had been such a long time since she had heard anyone call her by her name she had trouble remembering it. She sat silently watching them. Her eyes were hard. They were trained to be hard. She had survived for about sixteen years in this wilderness, for the most part alone.

'Don't you remember your name, girl?' Red Rivers lowered his arms and placed his hands on his knees. His actions were slow and carefully executed not to give her cause to use her weapon.

She shook her head.

'But you speak English?' Red looked at her young face, weathered by circumstance.

'I speak American like my folks did,' she said bluntly.

'They dead?'

'Ma went first when I was little,' she recalled, 'then Pa joined her in Heaven a few winters back.'

'What your pa call you?' Palomino asked, pouring himself a coffee.

'Nothing. He just said "You" and "Girl", or just whistled at me when he wanted something.' She was getting uneasy.

'You got a bible?' The Kid had an idea. If she knew of Heaven, she might just possess a bible.

'You mean a good book?' She seemed to get excited. 'Ma had a good book. She used to read me stories about folks who lived way off. Way past here in a place near Heaven.'

'Where's your ma's book?' Palomino asked the girl.

She pointed at a box near them. It was a box that had once been on a wagon. A box which had been well made by a craftsman many years ago.

'In the box,' she said, pointing the rifle barrel. 'It's in the box. Take a look.'

Kid Palomino opened the lid of the box and looked at the once-lovely clothes which now were little more than rags. He gently lifted the top layer and found the battered old book. Faded gold leaf lettering was embossed upon its leather cover: 'HOLY BIBLE'.

He turned back to face the girl with the book in his hands.

'May I open it and read?' he asked.

'Will you read me a story, pretty man?'

'Sure.'

She watched as he carefully opened the cover and

stared at the handwriting inside. There were numerous records of marriages and births listed going back over seventy years. He found the one entry he sought and read it aloud.

'To Jacob and Esme Patterson, a daughter Winifred Agnes born this day May 10th 1852.' The Kid looked up at her face as he finished.

'What?' She seemed unable to recognize the name.

'Maybe they called you Winnie?' Palomino suggested.

Her face lit up. She smiled and, for the first time since they had encountered her, lowered the rifle.

'Winnie.' Her eyes had tears in them. 'Ma called me Winnie. I remember that . . .'

'Hi, Winnie,' Red grinned.

'You want me to read you a story now?' Palomino asked in a low, quiet voice.

She nodded.

Both she and Red Rivers sat silently as Palomino read them a few pages from the old, battered bible. For the girl, it was the first time she had heard such words in over twelve years. Twelve hard years.

Suddenly she felt almost human again.

Seven

Matt Davis was an extremely large man. Unlike his brother he did not look fit or capable enough at holding his own in a brawl or shoot-out. Yet why should he? This was a man who had long ago ceased to do his own dirty work. Now he had enough money and power to get others to do his bidding. He had his own private army of gunmen – at least a dozen hired hands who did everything they were told. These men were cheap hired help. Cheap guns.

The one thing all Matt Davis' men had in common was their lack of spine. They were not thinkers, they were just the feeble-brained thugs he had imported over the past few years.

Loyal to a degree. These men knew that they earned more working for Matt Davis than any of them could earn with an honest employer. To them, taking their wages was proof of their loyalty.

To Davis, these were men he would send to do his bidding. If they got killed he simply went out and hired more. It was easy to get cheap gunmen, even here in the remote township of Badwater Creek.

All was not what it seemed, though.

Davis owned many things, including a gold-mine.

Yet none of these men seemed to work in Davis' legitimate business. These were just hired muscle.

If anyone did work in his gold-mine, it was not easy to find them in this town any longer. Once, half the men in Badwater Creek were employed at his gold-mine, yet that was then, not now.

Now, Matt Davis still gave the appearance of someone with gold nuggets in his safe, but exactly how did they get there?

Just what was the secret of Matt Davis' success?

Many had thought about that question over recent years, yet none had managed to figure it out.

Davis had an endless supply of money.

To employ so many gunmen, he had to have a lot of money. Yet where did it come from?

His saloons were busy. His 'soiled doves' brought in a lot of cash, but the books did not seem to balance. Only Matt Davis knew the answer for sure.

Yet he was the one man nobody had the guts to question.

It was starting to get slightly warmer in town as the sheriff entered the Lady G.

There was a look of concern upon his face. This was a very troubled man wearing the tin star.

Bob Davis made his way across the sawdust-covered floor, past the ineffective figure of Charlie the bartender, and through the door which read 'PRIVATE'.

Surrounded by four of his gunmen, Matt Davis looked up at his younger brother with little sign of interest in his eyes.

'Bob,' he muttered, as his teeth manoeuvred the thick imported cigar around his mouth. His grey hair was slicked down with pomade in a vain attempt to conceal his true age. he struck a match and rolled the thick Havana around, creating a cloud of smoke.

Whatever was troubling the junior Davis, it was unlikely to give the elder any sleepless nights.

The sheriff stood with his knuckles resting on his hips as he watched his brother go through the boring routine of lighting an expensive cigar.

'Matt?'

The elder Davis stared up at his brother, and then rested himself back in the expensive leather chair. He looked over the smoking length of the cigar at his sibling, with tired, baggy eyes.

'What you want, Bob?' he sighed. 'I'm busy.'

'You interested in what's going on around here?' Bob Davis asked as he leaned on the beautiful oak desk.

'Not unduly, brother.' Matt blew a thick cloud of smoke at the man wearing the tin star. A star that he had managed to acquire for his sibling. There was nothing better for a business man than having a tame lawman on the pay-roll. When that tame officer happened to be kin, it was ideal.

'What would you say if I told you the two strangers in town are Kid Palomino and Red Rivers?' Bob Davis tilted his head, so he could witness the expression upon his elder brother's face.

Matt Davis leaned forward and clenched his hands together.

'The lawmen from down south?'

'The same.'

'That does put a fox in my hen-house, brother.' Matt Davis chewed on the thick, brown tobacco, and puffed as he thought. It was like a train at a station taking on water. Even the hired guns moved away as the cloud grew thicker over their boss's head.

'The fires have got them boys interested, Matt.' Bob knew that his older brother must have something to do with the arson attacks around town, even if he had never been told officially.

'No matter.' The man rose to his feet and pushed his gunmen aside. He rounded the large desk and strode up to the taller, fitter Davis. He continued to chew on the cigar as his brain raced through endless thoughts. Thoughts that only he was privy to.

'But these guys are good. They'll cotton on.' Bob followed his brother up to the office window which looked out into an alley. 'If you're behind these fires, that is?'

'Cotton on? Cotton on to what?' Matt glanced at his brother as the smoke drifted up into his eyes. 'Why would I have anything to do with setting fire to folks' homes, brother?'

'They'll figure out what you're doing.' Bob gave a frustrated sigh.

'What am I doing, brother?'

'You're having folks burned out of their homes, Matt.'

'I think you are talking loco, Bob.' Matt grinned and removed the cigar from his dry lips. He flicked the grey ash onto the floor. 'Why would I do such a thing?'

The sheriff shrugged. He knew that he was right, but he also knew that nobody would ever get his brother to admit it.

'Hell, Matt. I'm just telling you to be careful.'

'I'm always careful.' Matt replaced the cigar into his mouth and took his hunter watch out from his vest pocket. The gold case sparkled in the sunlight that came in through the window. 'Go away and do something useful.'

The hired gunmen all started to laugh at the figure of the sheriff as he began to walk away from their boss.

'If Palomino and his buddy corner you, Matt,' he began, 'I might not be able to help you this time.'

'You'll help me brother. Just like all the other times.'

Eight

Winnie Patterson sat cross legged as she watched the two men opposite her. She had little experience of men.

At least not white men. The only white men she had met over the past few years had been gunning for her. Rivers and the Kid were different, and that confused her greatly.

Indian men she knew. She had long been friendly with the few Utes that frequented the forest and mountains. She traded with these men. They had known her when she was a small child, when they had first encountered the mountain man and his tiny daughter. That was many a long while ago.

Over the years, these Indians had gone out of their way to periodically check on her on the mountain. They brought her coffee and eggs, and she gave them furs. Not that they wanted her furs, but they knew that was all she had to trade with. They respected this young female for her courage. She remained up on the top of the mountain, digging for gold, which she never considered trading.

They thought she must have a small fortune in nuggets hidden away by now. Yet it was of no value either to them or her. She dug the gold because her father had dug the gold. He had died long before he had been able to explain to his daughter the reason for finding gold. She had indeed accumulated a lot of gold nuggets in the years since her father had passed away. She hid it as her father had hidden it.

The exact reasons why she went through this back-breaking routine were unknown to her. It was what she did.

Perhaps she hoped one day she would suddenly have an answer.

That day was closer than she expected.

To the Utes she was 'Little Huntress'. The one white person they not only trusted but respected. She had no fear of them and they had nothing but admiration and a little pity for her.

To Kid Palomino and Red Rivers she was Winnie Patterson, the girl who had forgotten her name. The girl who had caught them with the skill of a hunter. The young female who seemed to have no idea why she lived upon a mountain-top, except that she had always done so.

Palomino handed the bible into her hands.

'We ought to be going, Winnie.'

She looked distressed.

'Why are you going?'

Red rubbed his fingers over his hairy chin and gave a troubled look at his partner.

'We've gotta lot of business in town, Winnie.'

'Stay,' she said, looking at the now clear sky overhead. 'You stay with me.'

Palomino started to get cautiously to his feet and helped his friend up. Red was stiff from sitting on the hard ground for so long, and almost creaked with the effort.

'We will come back.' He smiled at the small female. 'I promise.'

She stood, and the bear skin dropped to the ground behind her.

'OK.'

'I'll read to you again,' the Kid smiled.

'Why did you come up here?' she asked as she pulled the guns from her jeans and returned them. 'Nobody comes up here any more. Not good folks anyway.'

'We are investigating a couple of fires in the valley down below, Winnie.'

'I see fires.' She nodded as the trio walked through the long grass toward the two mounts who were grazing.

'You thought we were claim-jumpers, didn't you?' Red asked the small girl.

'Yes.'

'Who has tried to jump your claim before?' Palomino questioned quietly.

'Men on horses like you,' she replied. 'Except they

were not pretty like you.'

'You know their names?' Palomino blushed.

'No.'

Rivers looked at his partner before turning to Winnie.

'You know where Matt Davis got his gold-mine?'

She stopped in her tracks. She recognized the name.

'Matt Davis? I know that man.'

Palomino stopped and gazed down into her face. She looked upset by memories connected with the name of Matt Davis.

'What's Matt Davis done to make you remember him so well, Winnie?'

'He killed my pa,' she retorted angrily.

'Why did he do that?'

'Pa would not sell our mine to him.' Winnie shuddered as her mind remembered things she had long since forced into the darkness of her brain. 'Davis came one day with lots of men and they killed my pa.'

'Why would Davis want your mine when he had one of his own?' the Kid wondered aloud.

'His mine got no more gold left,' Winnie explained.

'But your gold-mine has still got gold?' Red looked around at the cliff-face, wondering where it was.

'They never knew where our mine was. They couldn't find it. They gave up looking after a while.' She was grinning. 'They could not find me either.'

'So your mine ain't up here?'

'Only the Indians and me know exactly where my claim is.' She looked down at the thousands of trees below them, and waved her arm. 'It's in there someplace.'

'How come the Indians know?' Red took off his hat and scratched his thinning hair.

'You can trust Indians,' she said bluntly.

'How come?' Red asked curiously.

'Indians never rob you.' She smiled at the scruffy man as he replaced his battered Stetson. 'Didn't you know that?'

'Is your mine registered, Winnie?' The Kid wondered how legal her rights were.

'What does that mean?' She looked puzzled.

'Did your pa have a legal piece of paper?'

'I think so. In the box.' She pointed back to her camp site.

Kid Palomino whistled to his mount Nugget. The beautiful stallion raised his head from the grass and started to walk toward them slowly.

Red Rivers whistled at his brown quarter-horse. Derby looked up briefly, then resumed his grazing.

'My horse is smarter than your horse,' Palomino grinned.

Red started to walk after his horse, muttering to himself as he waded through the tall grass.

Kid Palomino took hold of Nugget's reins and rubbed the white flame that ran down the horse's nose. Winnie seemed interested in the beautiful horse, yet nervous of its great size.

'This is Nugget.' Palomino introduced his horse to the female who looked up at it. 'And Nugget, this is my dear friend Winnie.'

'Nugget?' She said softly as her hand reached out to touch the creature's warm nose. 'I have lots of gold nuggets.'

Palomino watched as his partner finally managed to gather up his reins and started to lead the quarter-horse back toward them.

'You never told us where Matt Davis' mine is located, Winnie.'

'Down that way. Right at the end of the rock-face.' She pointed past her small camp. 'The Indians helped me hide from the men with the guns. We picked a few of them off as they tried to get me.'

Red drew up to the others and stopped. He was panting with exhaustion.

'I gotta teach this dang horse to come when I whistle,' he grumbled. 'My feet is too old for all this walking.'

Palomino put his left foot in the stirrup and hoisted himself up into the saddle. She stood looking up at him.

'You wanna get up on back?'

She looked at the horse again and was unsure.

'I . . . I think so but . . .'

The Kid leaned down, put his hand under the pit of her shoulder and raised her up. She scrambled her legs until they were on either side of the horse. Her arms gripped his middle tightly. Very tightly. He was surprised at her strength and had to prise them a little looser.

'Now you can direct us to that gold-mine of Mr Matt Davis.'

'I'm scared,' she stammered. 'It's very high up here.'

'But look at the view, Winnie,' Palomino laughed. 'Look at the wonderful view.'

'She gotta open her eyes first, Kid,' Red laughed.

Nine

It was early evening as the two riders headed back toward Badwater Creek. As the sun fell below the tree and mountain lines a red glow silently lost its nightly battle with the ensuing blackness of the night. Soon the sky was alive with twinkling stars above their heads. Kid Palomino had not spoken to his partner since they had left the young Winnie Patterson up on the top of the windswept mountain.

They had seen the deserted gold-mine which belonged to Matt Davis and could tell by its condition that nobody had worked there for years.

Kid Palomino sat in his saddle, allowing the stallion to walk at its own pace. He was thinking. The trouble was, none of this made any sense. Nothing he had learned seemed to make him any wiser.

There had to be a reason behind all this, yet it was as if everything, from the fires to the gold-mine and the silver deposits, were unconnected.

They had to be connected, Palomino reasoned.

What was the connection?

He continued to let Nugget walk at his own pace as he sat in his saddle restlessly.

Red Rivers looked ahead at the street-lights of town. They were about a quarter of a mile ahead along the narrow trail. Then he turned his attention upon his partner. The younger man was silent and mulling over the facts in his mind. Facts that were so very complicated that they seemed to defy explanation.

By Kid Palomino's expression, he was getting no closer to the truth.

'What you reckon is going on here, Kid?' Red asked as he rubbed his chin-hair.

Palomino gave Red a thoughtful glance.

'This is the strangest darn situation we have ever found ourselves in,' the Kid sighed. 'I have been thinking about all the things we have been faced with since we arrived here, and for the life of me, I am no smarter.'

'We could lit out in the morning, Kid.'

'We could.' The Kid leaned against the castle of his saddle and stared ahead at the lights of Badwater Creek as they grew closer. 'But we ain't gonna.'

'Why?'

'I'd never sleep again if I don't figure this out.' Palomino had an itch in his curiosity and had to find a way of scratching it. The itch made him wonder why houses were being torched to the ground, and what a rich man who owned a useless gold-mine wanted with another man's claim.

'It is rather frustrating.' Rivers steered Derby around the bend and headed past the first buildings of the small town.

'Frustrating?' the Kid laughed. 'I'm getting a headache.'

'Maybe we ought to—'

'Forget Wyoming.' Kid Palomino pulled his Stetson down over his eyes. 'I ain't going no place until I've worked this out.'

'That was what I thought you'd say, Palomino.' Red shook his weary head and followed his friend up to the hitching pole outside Doc Jenkins' place. His tired eyes focused on his friend intently.

Kid Palomino dismounted and stepped up onto the porch, his spurs making a jangling noise as he walked.

'You coming in?' the Kid asked his older pal as he reached the door.

Red shook his head and remained in his saddle as he watched his friend knocking on the door frame.

The door opened and a small, plump lady answered. She had a friendly disposition about her. She looked like the ideal aunt or mother of your dreams.

'Hello. You must be Kid Palomino. My husband had to go out on a call. He said it would be all right for you to see Lucy for a few minutes.' Her voice was high pitched and frail, yet charming all the same.

'I'm a bit dusty, ma'am,' the Kid apologized for his appearance.

76

'Don't you fret none.' She smiled understandingly.

Palomino removed his hat and tossed it up to his partner, before entering the building behind the small lady.

'She's in here.' Mrs Jenkins opened a door to a room where Lucy Hall sat in a chair. 'Lucy? You have a visitor.'

Kid Palomino bowed in gratitude to the small woman and entered the room. He ambulated toward the padded chair where Lucy Hall waited with a smile on her face. As he sat down on a hard-backed chair near her, he saw the older woman disappear from view out of the corner of his eye.

Lucy looked tired as she sat with her white dressing-gown wrapped around her. He could see the iodine stains on her lower legs and wondered how extensive her burns had been. His own were still sore, but they were nothing compared to hers.

'So you came back after all?' Lucy smiled.

'I had to see how you were, Miss Hall.' He looked down at the floor.

'You have earned the right to call me Lucy.' She patted his hand with her red fingers. Her touch made the young man look away from her. He liked what he saw, but was never easy around female company.

'I didn't do much, Lucy.' He blushed.

'You saved my life, Palomino,' she said weakly. 'You could have let me burn, but you risked your own skin for a total stranger. Why?'

'Why?' He thought for a moment before shrugging. 'I guess I ain't got an answer for you, Lucy.'

'I think you have . . .' She might have been weak but she knew that this man had something in his past which made him what he was. Her stare was aimed straight at his face. He had nowhere to hide.

'You're right, Lucy,' he admitted. 'A long time ago I lost my family in a house fire.'

'How awful.' She could see it tortured him to remember that sad event, and leaned forward to take his hand in hers once more. This time she held on to it. 'You were young?'

'I was just a little kid.' He put his hand to his face to hide the emotion he knew was revealing itself. 'I was at school, and when I got home . . .'

'I understand.' Lucy Hall now understood how a perfect stranger could risk his own life trying to save another's.

'You might, but I don't,' he shrugged.

He got to his feet and turned his back on her as he moved to the window. He was not looking out of it, he was trying to compose himself. Memories had entered his mind of times he had long chosen to forget. For a moment as he stood upright he felt a pain. The pain of recollection.

'Your burns OK?' he croaked.

'Getting better.'

'That's good.' He took a huge gulp of air and moved to a lamp perched on a wooden desk. Lifting the glass, he struck a match and put it to the wick.

The flame rose high before he replaced the glass. His thin fingers adjusted the control of the lamp until it was at its brightest. The room was now bathed in a soft, warm light as he returned to her again. He could see how pretty she was, for a woman of her age. He figured she was at least thirty, and that was old for a woman not to have a husband in these parts.

'You know who wants your land?' he asked.

'Nobody wants my old piece of land, Palomino.'

'You're wrong, Lucy.' He moved toward her. 'Your land has silver deposits on it.'

'What?' She looked shocked. 'Are you sure?'

'Yep. Didn't you notice the blue sludge everywhere?'

'That muck is silver?' She raised an eyebrow. 'I had no idea. It's been a real nuisance.'

'But valuable.' He grinned. 'Very valuable, Lucy.'

'But why burn me out?' She was intrigued.

'If I knew the answer to that, I'd have this problem licked already.' He moved closer.

She stared up at his lean body. The close-fitting clothes that showed there wasn't an ounce of fat on his entire body. The pair of matched Colt Peacemakers in their hand-tooled holsters. The black, expensive boots. Then she looked up at his face. A good face. An honest face that seemed out of place in this town. The face of a man who had saved her life.

'You seem convinced that there is a sinister plot behind my house fire, Palomino,' she uttered. Her eyes were fixed upon his face.

He glanced down.

'Yep. I'll figure it out,' he said, touching his forehead and turning. 'When I do, someone is going to pay.'

'You're going?' She seemed saddened.

As he reached the door he stopped momentarily to look back at her once more. She looked like an angel as she sat there, he thought. Men have no right to go near angels.

'Take it easy, Lucy. Rest like Doc Jenkins said.' Palomino hesitated for an instant, before continuing.

As she heard the front door close behind him, Lucy Hall looked up at the ceiling and lay back in her chair. Its padded seat comforted her body, but her mind was confused by this heroic man who had saved her life.

A tear rolled from the corner of her eye as she lay there. She had no idea why.

Ten

The streets were quiet and dark. The street-lights were spaced a long way apart, and the result was long shadows everywhere.

They intended to find out a few things tonight. The problem was, Matt Davis' touch seemed to reach everywhere.

Both Kid Palomino and Red Rivers were dog-tired. This was a strange place. Now, as darkness reigned supreme, it actually seemed to be getting warmer.

Then they turned a corner and saw the Lady G Saloon once more ahead of them.

The noise drifted out into the street before them. An out-of-tune piano was playing somewhere within the drinking-hole. It sounded as if the player had ten thumbs.

'You thirsty, Red?' Palomino pulled both Colts from their holsters and checked the impressive pistols. Both were still loaded to maximum. Twirling them back into their resting-places when satisfied they were operational, the Kid rubbed the palms of his hands on his shirt.

'I could handle a beer, Kid,' Rivers grinned. It was as if he could read his partner's thoughts. He knew Palomino would rather drink coffee than beer, but he followed.

Kid Palomino led the way down the boardwalk and into the saloon. It was crowded. They made their way toward the bar where they spied Charlie serving. Kid Palomino rested one boot on the brass rail and leaned forward.

The crowd was entirely masculine. There was a card game going on in a corner, and men were gathered around a long table playing dice. Most looked like ordinary folks, but a few seemed different.

The piano was still being played badly in the corner. It hardly mattered, as the voices occasionally drowned out the sound of the ivories.

Palomino knew his back was covered by his experienced partner as he leaned onto the counter and silently raised a finger to the bartender.

Rivers stood behind the Kid with his eyes studying everyone in the room, their backs almost touching as they stood together. This was a team. Two men who had cleaned up many a mess by acting as one, in perfect unison.

It was rare to find a partner that you could trust with your life. Both men knew they were lucky.

Charlie cautiously approached them.

'What you troublemakers want this time?'

'Two beers,' Palomino answered.

The bartender quickly pulled two draughts of suds and plonked them before the Kid. Palomino tossed a coin at the man and then handed one of the glasses backward to his pal.

It seemed that all eyes were on them as they stood drinking their beers. They watched the scene with eyes that were trained in the art of spotting trouble. It didn't take long before they saw what they were looking for.

Three men in a corner. One with a bandage wrapped tightly around his left hand. A bandage that had a dark bloodstain on it.

Kid Palomino nudged his partner and knew that it was pretty certain that these were the men who had bushwhacked them at Old Man Smith's place earlier.

The three men looked uneasy as Palomino and Red started to walk through the crowd toward them. They seemed as if they were about to make a run for the door, but decided against such an obvious admission of guilt.

Unknown to them, the approaching duo were deadly serious.

The Kid and Rivers cornered the three men, who were sitting at a table with a half-bottle of rye before them. These three men were indeed part of Matt Davis' bunch of hired hands. The oldest called himself 'Reno', another was known as 'Black-haired Joe', and the one with the bandaged left hand was simply called 'Dwan'.

'Howdy, boys,' Palomino smiled, touching the brim of his Stetson.

'Get lost.' Reno seemed nervous.

Palomino smiled at his partner before looking directly into Reno's bloodshot eyes.

'Why you trying to upset me, Mister?'

Reno's hand went for his gun, only to have Kid Palomino's boot kick it swiftly. The man winced in agony and raised his hand up to his mouth. He gritted his teeth and glared angrily at the tall figure of Kid Palomino.

'You better get out of this town, dude,' Reno snarled.

The two other men seemed ready to join in, until they noticed Red had his hand on the handle of his .45. They simmered down quickly.

'Let's get out of here, Reno,' Dwan advised his companion.

Kid Palomino moved to the man who spoke and stared at his bandaged hand.

'Hurt yourself?'

'Cut himself shaving, Palomino,' Red chuckled.

'Uh . . .' The man was unsure what to say and glanced frantically around his friends for assistance. None was forthcoming.

Kid Palomino swiftly grabbed the bandaged hand and lifted it up. The gunman cried out in pain, as he was being held by his wounded wrist. He was helpless.

'I reckon you got a bullet in this hand, friend,' Palomino remarked. 'One of mine?'

'Let go! Let go!' The man screamed.

Palomino did not release his grip. He watched the other two men as he finished his beer and rested the empty glass onto the table.

'You boys stink of something . . .'

'Smells like coal-oil to me, Palomino,' Red nodded.

'That's it. Coal-oil.' The Kid grinned as Dwan still pleaded for his wounded hand to be released. The begging fell on deaf ears. The room was silent. Fifty men all watching five men in a corner. 'How come you critters smell of coal-oil?'

'What you talking about coal-oil for?' Reno snarled at the Kid. 'You're loco.'

'We don't know nothing about no coal-oil,' Black-haired Joe chipped in.

'Seems to me you boys been having yourselves a little fun setting fire to other folks's houses,' Palomino grinned through gritted teeth.

'Prove it,' Reno grunted.

Palomino twisted Dwan's hand again, pressing his thumbnail into the bloodstain. This time it worked.

'We did it! We did it!' Dwan screamed out loud.

Kid Palomino released the man's wounded hand and stared at the other two.

'Guess that could be called proof, Reno.' He smiled.

'You're dead men,' Black-haired Joe snarled as he pushed his chair backward in the sawdust. He sat glaring from his seat at Palomino.

Kid Palomino squared himself to face both Joe and Reno as he stood behind the sobbing figure of Dwan.

Red Rivers moved beside his partner and stopped smiling as his hand rested on the handle of his gun.

Unlike Red, the Kid held his hands a few inches above his pistols. His long thin fingers were outstretched and poised for action.

'I suggest you take your guns out of your holsters, boys.'

'You're dead!' Reno boomed.

Kid Palomino's eyes narrowed as he focused like an eagle upon its prey.

'I'd think long and hard about your next move, Reno.'

Reno gave the sobbing Dwan a nervous look before realizing that after taking a kick from the Kid's size-12 boot, his shooting hand was not in a very reliable state.

'Place your irons on the table.' Red had both eyes almost shut as he concentrated on his chosen target. In situations such as these, he and the Kid had long since worked out which man they would draw on. Red had drawn Reno. Palomino had drawn Black-haired Joe. That was the way it would be.

Reno glanced between Rivers and the Kid. A flicker of doubt was starting to cross his face as he sat next to Joe. He was rubbing the bruised hand anxiously.

'Wait on,' Reno piped up. 'I still got a dead hand

here from that kicking.'

'That ought to make it easier for me,' Red voiced.

'I mean . . .' Reno looked across to his right and Black-haired Joe. 'Not now, Joe. This is stupid.'

Black-haired Joe suddenly realized that he was facing two gunfighters alone and outnumbered if Reno was not going to join in.

'What you mean, Reno?' Joe questioned.

'They got the drop on us,' Reno admitted. 'We ain't gonna win this one.'

Black-haired Joe's face went pale. Suddenly he was aware of his own vulnerability.

'You chicken-livered . . .' He spat his words of contempt towards Reno and shook his head woefully.

'Two fingers,' Palomino said. 'Take them guns out with two fingers and place them on the table. Nice and easy.'

The three gunmen complied with their instructions.

Red gathered up the pistols.

Eleven

Sheriff Bob Davis was almost asleep in his chair as the office door was noisily opened. He rubbed his eyes in disbelief as Reno entered, holding his arms above his head. Getting to his feet, Bob Davis then watched as Dwan and Black-haired Joe followed.

Kid Palomino stood in the doorway next to Red Rivers, their guns aimed at the three gunmen. Red pulled out the three pistols belonging to their prisoners and dropped them onto the desk, where he rested his rump.

'What you doing?' Davis ranted as he approached the Kid.

'Put these varmints in a cell, Sheriff,' Palomino ordered.

'What for?' The sheriff yelled.

'Arson and murder,' Palomino answered.

Bob Davis cleared his throat, thinking of his brother. This looked bad. Matt would be pretty mad about this, he thought.

'Who they kill?'

'Old Man Smith for one.' Red smiled at the law officer.

'Smith is dead?' Davis glanced at the three men, who still held their arms high above their heads.

'Yep,' the Kid quipped. 'And they did it.'

'You got any proof?'

'The wounded skunk admitted it in the saloon. I figure we got a lot of witnesses.' Palomino sighed, staring at the sheriff as he reluctantly herded the three men into the first cell.

They watched as the key locked the cell door. As Bob Davis moved back toward the two strangers, they made their way out of the door and out into the dark street.

'Where are you two going?' Davis shouted after them.

Kid Palomino paused for a second and gave the man a cold stare that hit its mark.

'Keep them men locked up, Sheriff. The circuit judge will be in town in three days,' Kid Palomino informed the man behind the badge.

'How do you know that?' Davis yelled. For the first time in a long while, he was scared, scared to death.

'I know a lot of things,' Palomino said. 'Like where the nearest marshal is right now.'

'Come back here, boys!' Davis yelled.

The two men continued walking away from the sheriff's office into the darkness. Neither man answered.

Neither man spoke for a few minutes after leaving

the three bushwhackers in the cold sheriff's office. They walked past store after store along the uneven boardwalks until they reached the hotel.

Then across at the stage depot they noticed the evening stagecoach being readied.

'What you thinking about?' Red asked his partner, who was rubbing his chin.

The Kid glanced at his pal and smiled.

'You go over to the stage and don't let them leave until I get back to you.'

Red ran across to the stage depot as the Kid walked inside the hotel lobby.

After a short while, the crumpled Red Rivers, who was standing next to the ox-like stagecoach driver, saw his friend striding toward them with a letter in his hand. Palomino handed the letter to the driver along with a dollar.

'Put this in your mail bag,' he instructed the driver.

'Sure thing,' the big man grinned at the Kid.

The two watched as the driver climbed up onto the high seat and gathered up his reins.

He released the brake and whipped the leather thongs down hard across the six-horse team. The stagecoach rolled out of Badwater Creek quickly.

'Who are you sending a letter, Kid?' Red asked, as they made their way back toward the hotel.

As the pair entered the bright lobby they slowed to shake off some of the day's dust.

'US Marshal Dobbs,' Palomino finally replied.

'What you writing to him for?' Red removed his old hat and shook his head.

Kid Palomino did not reply to his friend. He knew that they might require the services of their old friend Ray Dobbs, whom they had worked with for over ten months the previous year. Dobbs was an honest marshal in Colorado, and quite a rarity.

Try as he might, the Kid could not shake off the feeling that he and his partner were headed for a show-down, with even the law against them.

As they took their room key and headed up the stairs slowly, they began to wonder how Matt Davis would take having three of his men in jail. The trouble was, he had a lot more men than that in town. These men were still free, and neither he nor Red had any idea what any of the others looked like.

'I'm tuckered out, Kid,' Red said, yawning as they entered their room.

Palomino struck a match and lit the lamp before closing the door. He moved to the fireplace and tossed the still-burning match into the already-prepared grate. The flames soon rose around the carefully arranged logs.

'You say you're tired, Red?' the Kid asked as he tossed his Stetson onto the easy chair.

Rivers had already stripped down to his pink long underwear, and was stretching beside his bed.

'Plumb tuckered.'

'Get some sleep,' Palomino nodded as he sat on the bed, leaning against the pillows. Soon his partner was snoring loudly, enjoying his overdue slumber. Kid Palomino sat watching the lights of the fire-flames reflecting around the room with hypnotic colour.

He lay for hours unable to relax enough to sleep. Somehow he had to find out what was going on in this small, remote part of the Colorado territories.

Then he thought about the frail, delicate Lucy Hall as he had seen her that evening.

Just like an angel. Even an angel couldn't fly with singed wings, he thought.

Then his thoughts finally became dreams.

Twelve

It was midnight when Matt Davis was cornered in the Lady G Saloon by Warren Stone.

Stone was a fat man. He always wore black, and had owned the town bank for several years. Despite giving the appearance of respectability, he was one of the most frequent visitors to Davis' other drinking hole, the Red Garter.

Stone was not a regular at the Red Garter for its alcoholic refreshment, but for the several women who worked there. Women who were paid for their services.

Services that had little to do with religious worship, but more to do with pressing the flesh. This was the only place in town where lonely men could find 'soiled doves': women willing to consider any proposal, as long at they could charge a fee for supplying it.

Warren Stone was indeed the most regular of visitors to the Red Garter, because he could not resist indulging in everything these ladies supplied.

Being a very rich man also helped him afford his vices.

Stone knew every female in the place so well that he had to ration how many times a week he would see each one. After all, it was pointless getting to know them as well as he knew his wife.

She was the only creature who did not get him interested, and if he ever thought of any of the Red Garter girls in that way, it would ruin his evenings.

Warren Stone had marched across the sawdusted floor of the half-empty saloon and pounded on the door to Matt Davis' private office.

'Matt?' Stone shouted at full volume.

The door quickly opened and the man who resembled an obese undertaker entered. The five or six gunmen who surrounded their employer moved aside as Stone approached.

"What the hell do you want, Stone?' Matt Davis seemed glued to his chair as the gunhands encircled the visitor.

'We gotta talk in private, Matt,' Stone insisted, looking with distaste at the men who hovered around Davis like flies around a cesspool.

Matt Davis' face grew animated as he waved his hand around at the gang. One by one they left the room, until only a gangly gunman named Johnson remained with the sweating Warren Stone.

Johnson was the sort of man who did what he was told. If he was ordered to go deaf, he would obey.

'What the hell are you so worked up about, Stone?'

Stone rubbed the back of his neck and seated himself opposite the imposing Davis.

'I just got news from the assay office up at Cheyenne.'

Davis sat forward.

'Go on,' he smiled.

'The silver in Badwater Creek ain't worth mining.' Stone tossed a paper at his friend. 'Look at the report. It is low-grade, and we wouldn't be able to afford to pay miners enough to make a profit.'

Davis read the note with a still expression on his face, before looking up at the man who sat before him across the desk.

'This ruins everything, Stone,' he grimaced, screwing the note up in his hand before tossing it onto the floor.

'Your big plans have blown up in our faces, Matt.'

Davis rose to his feet and shook with anger as he moved to his silver-plated cigar box. He opened the box and picked up a large Havana. Biting off the end, he struck a match and lit the weed.

Staring through the cloud of smoke, he paced around the room before stopping at Stone's side. He looked down at the nervous banker with venom in his eyes.

'So now we got a couple of burned-out houses around town and a dead body?' Davis spat out a tobacco leaf at the floor. 'But our major problem still exists.'

'I told you we couldn't get away with it.' Stone sat with his hands clenched. The veins in the back of his hands were swollen and blue. 'I ought never to have listened to you, Matt. It was a crazy idea.'

'It was a good idea. It still is.' Davis inhaled the thick smoke that burned his throat.

'Embezzlement of bank funds was and still is crazy, Matt.'

'But we did it, didn't we?' Matt Davis ran his hand along the back of Stone's hard chair. 'You seemed all right with the idea at the time.'

Stone started to get to his feet, when two strong hands forced him back down.

'I went along with your plan because—'

'We both know why you agreed to my little plan, Warren.' Davis paced around and sat on the lip of the desk staring hard at the sweating man. 'So it's gone sour on us. So what?'

'So what?' Stone was edgy. 'We have stolen bank funds worth tens of thousands of dollars, and your men have committed murder, Matt. If that gets out, they'll lynch us.'

Matt Davis sucked on the thick brown cigar slowly as he studied his accomplice. He was looking at the weak link in his chain. This was a man who had to be calmed down.

'Why are you so worked up, Stone?' he asked.

'I heard that there are two lawmen in town.'

Stone gushed with emotion as he spoke.

'Kid Palomino and his partner.' Davis filled in the names.

'They have arrested three of your men.'

'And put them in my brother's jail, Stone.' Davis grinned at his guest. 'I'll get them out tomorrow.'

'But—'

'No problem.' Davis blew a line of smoke at the ceiling as he rubbed his stiff neck. 'Palomino is just a drifter in Badwater Creek. I can get him arrested and hung if I wanna.'

Stone looked a little more relaxed as he sat before the confident, smoking man.

'What about the silver?'

'If your expert says it ain't worth digging, then we leave it where it is.' Davis was thoughtful. 'I still got a gold-mine after all.'

'But you said that ain't got enough gold in it to fill a tooth,' Stone remembered.

'True.' Davis grinned as he picked up his bottle of rye off the table and poured out two glasses-full. He indicated to Stone, who picked up one of the glasses and swallowed it quickly.

'What good is a worthless gold-mine?' Stone asked.

'There is gold on that mountain, Stone.' He nodded as he sipped at his drink. 'A lot of gold. The trouble is, it belongs to a crazy mountain girl. All I gotta do is get her gold and we can clear up all our debts and have a good profit with the leftovers.'

'I thought you said you had tried before to find out where that kid's mine is, Matt.' Stone reached for the bottle and poured himself another. 'Without success.'

'That was before.' Davis finished his rye and placed the empty glass on the desk. 'It was different then.'

'What is different now?' Stone enquired.

'Now I'll try a little harder. I think I'll get my boys to take a lot of dynamite up there to my mine and be a little careless. If they blow up enough of that mountain they just might find something.' Matt Davis wandered back to his chair and sat down. Johnson was still standing motionless by the wall.

'You would blow up an entire mountain?' Stone gasped.

'If I have to.' Matt Davis waved a hand at Johnson, who moved closer. 'Get the boys and take a pack-mule up to the gold-mine, and blow it off the face of the mountain.'

'When?' Johnson fingered his chin.

'Now.' Davis glared at the man. The man nodded and left the office.

Stone finished his drink and got to his feet without looking at the man in front of him. He knew that whatever he said, the man would have something else to add. That was one thing about Matt Davis. He had strength of character.

Nothing affected him.

Nothing frightened him.

Warren Stone headed for the office door that led back into the heart of the Lady G Saloon.

'Stop worrying, Stone,' Davis advised, in a tone that almost insisted on compliance.

Stone glanced at the man seated behind the big desk as he left the office. He was heading home this night. The girls at the Red Garter would lose their best customer this evening.

Worry can affect different men in different ways, and worry had made Warren Stone feel anything but amorous. He dragged his feet through the thick sawdust on the saloon floor, and headed out into the night air.

The evening air was chilly as he pulled up the collar of his coat to cover his fat neck.

As he walked, he thought of all the thousands of dollars he had spent. Dollars that belonged to the town's citizens. Dollars that he had spent on women. Dollars that he should have left in his safe. Then he thought of all the money he had given to Matt Davis for his schemes.

Schemes that included building a business empire. The trouble was, the dream of a business empire was built upon very shaky ground.

They had created a castle made of cards.

One gust of wind could bring it all crashing down around their ears. His footsteps echoed around the quiet streets as he slowly made his way home.

Warren Stone was a very worried soul.

He pushed open the gate and made his way up

the flower-lined pathway to the front door. There on the porch sat Dale Cody, the assayer from Cheyenne. Cody was a skinny man who sported a thin moustache and wore his sideburns long. His Stetson covered his oiled dark hair.

Cody stayed in the shadows as the large man approached him.

'How did it go, Stone?' Cody asked with interest.

'He swallowed it.' Stone sat beside the young man and wiped his face free of perspiration.

'You convinced him the silver was low-grade?'

'Yes, and it wasn't easy, Cody.'

'You must be a pretty fine actor, my friend,' Cody laughed, and slapped his knee in glee.

Stone gave a sigh of relief.

'I'm scared,' he admitted. 'Matt Davis ain't the sort of guy you can cross.'

'Matt Davis is finished in this town, Stone.' Dale Cody leaned forward and smacked one hand into the palm of another with a wry smile on his face. 'Pretty soon it'll be just you and me.'

Stone felt the sweat soaking into his undershirt as he nodded in agreement.

'This plan of yours better work, for both our sakes.'

Dale Cody got to his feet and drew his pistol from its holster before checking its action.

'I got a few things to do,' he said, sliding the gun back into its leather sheath. 'I'll get back to you.'

Stone watched as the man slipped away into the

darkness of the street and blended in with the shadows. He gulped, and wondered if he had made the correct decision.

It was too late to fret.

Thirteen

It was about 4.30 in the morning when the firing started. It lasted only a matter of seconds but the noise caused panic in the town, which was still under the influence of darkness.

Kid Palomino awoke from his deep slumber fully dressed, and rushed to the window of his hotel room. He stared out, but could see nothing in the dimly illuminated street.

Red Rivers sat upright in his bed and gazed across at his partner at the window.

'What is it?' he yawned.

Palomino tossed his friend's clothes to him.

'Get dressed. Quick!'

Rivers fumbled with the clothing as he lowered his legs onto the floor.

'What's up?'

'I heard shots,' Palomino answered.

'So what?'

'They came from the direction of the jail.'

Rivers dressed and strapped on his gunbelt.

'You sure?'

'Nope.' Palomino put on his hat and handed Red his as they left the peace of Room 20. 'I wanna check, all the same.'

The two men moved quickly down the staircase and through the lobby. They arrived in the street to see men coming from the Lady G Saloon in earnest.

Everyone seemed to be heading for the jail and Bob Davis' sheriff's office.

Palomino and Red looked at one another before walking in the same direction themselves. They arrived after the crowd had gathered in the small building, but still managed to force their way through.

The sight that confronted them was hideous in its brutality, and even hardened gunmen were turning away from the sight.

Kid Palomino pushed his hat back on his head as he took a couple of deep breaths of air. His eyes rolled over the scene before him. It was not a pretty sight.

Red shook his head, sighing.

On the floor next to his desk Bob Davis' body lay. A single hole in the centre of his forehead was still pumping blood onto the wooden boards. It was as if even in death the heart had to keep pumping blood until there was nothing left to pump.

In the cell, Reno, Black-haired Joe and Dwan were also dead in their beds. Blood from their wounds still dripped from the cots onto the cell floor. The red pool seemed to grow with every passing second.

Kid Palomino rubbed the back of his neck as he tried to figure out what had occured.

The cell door was still locked tight and the keys hung on a peg near the desk.

'Whoever done this was a darn good shot,' Red observed, as he peered into the cell through the bars. 'I can see but one shot per body in there.'

'You mean this was a four-shot deal?' the Kid quizzed his partner.

'Yep. Looks like one bullet each.' Red continued to shake his head.

'Where them critters hit?' Palomino moved cautiously to the cell.

'Head shots,' Red answered. 'Each one in the head.'

Kid Palomino was stunned. Whoever had entered this office had coldly executed four men by accurately shooting each one in the head.

'That's accuracy, Kid.' Red Rivers rubbed his beard as they turned to the other people in the jail building.

At that moment, the crowd of men parted and the heavy figure of Matt Davis strode toward them. His face was white as he moved past both Palomino and Rivers to the body of his sibling.

They watched as he kneeled down beside the still-warm body.

For a moment the man was silent, then he rose to his feet and turned toward the Kid and Rivers.

'Who did this?' Davis yelled at the crowd.

'Whoever did this, he was one heck of a shot,' Palomino said, as the burly Davis moved closer to him.

Matt Davis stared up into the pale blue eyes of the Kid and searched for an answer. There was none there.

'Do you know anything about this?'

'Nope,' Palomino replied.

'You're Kid Palomino, ain't you?'

'I ain't made no secret of that fact, Mr Davis.'

'You know me?'

'Only by reputation. The way you know me.'

Davis turned away for a second as he suddenly realized how upset he was by his brother's death. He then moved to the cell and stared at the three bodies. Each had been his men. He owned them the way he owned everything else. They had belonged to him. Now they were dead, like his younger brother.

It made no sense.

'Who would kill these men?' he mumbled in disbelief to himself. There seemed to be no logical answer.

'Whoever it was is a real good shot, Mr Davis,' Rivers said, pointing at the centre of his own forehead. 'That ain't an easy shot.'

'Especially four times in succession,' Palomino added.

Matt Davis leaned down, picked up his brother's body in his arms and walked out of the jailhouse through the crowd. Palomino noticed the blood-soaked knees of the infamous Matt Davis' pants.

Kid Palomino gave his friend a glance. Nothing was said.

Fourteen

Neither Palomino nor Rivers spoke for over an hour as they sat in Room 20 of the hotel. It was almost six in the morning, and getting colder by the minute. An icy breeze had drifted over the top of the nearby mountains and continued to keep the chill on the fertile valley and small township of Badwater Creek.

Kid Palomino pulled the service cord near the fireplace and returned to the window.

'What you ring for?' Red asked, shivering on his bed.

'For someone to make up the fire again,' Palomino retorted.

Red Rivers nodded gratefully.

The pair sat watching their body heat turn to vapour as they exhaled toward each other.

'Wyoming must be colder than this.' The Kid raised an eyebrow as he watched his friend. 'Makes you think.'

'Colder than this?' Red looked painfully at his pal. 'How do you figure that?'

'Wyoming is further north, ain't it?'

'Is it?' Red pulled the sheets around his shoulders as he shook on the bed springs.

'I bet Texas is just about right.' Palomino smiled.

'The Panhandle must be darn sweaty right about now,' Red concurred.

The bedroom door opened, and the beautiful figure of young Annie Brown entered. As was her usual rule, she did not bother to knock.

Both men watched as she moved toward them. She seemed to float across the carpet. Her face was as blank as ever.

'Walker said the bell rang.' She spoke in pinched words, as if she was being charged for every sentence.

Palomino pointed to the cold grate.

'If you could make up the fire again, Annie?'

'OK.' She left the room as silently as she had entered.

The two men sat on their beds, staring at each other. The evening had been nothing if not strange.

'Who would have killed Davis and the three gunslingers?' Red directed a cold glance at his friend.

'Certainly not Davis Senior.' Palomino smiled thoughtfully.

'It doesn't figure.'

'Name one thing that does figure.' Palomino watched as the door opened again. Annie carried a huge metal bucket to the fireplace and kneeled down. She silently prepared the grate for a fresh fire.

'What connection has little Winnie Patterson to all this, Palomino?' Red asked his friend.

The Kid shook his head as if unable to put anything together that would make any sense.

'Beats me, Red,' he admitted. 'I feel sorry for the girl, stuck on that mountain. All alone.'

Red agreed.

'Yep. The girl don't seem to know what to do.'

'Would you?' Palomino wondered.

'I doubt it, Kid.' Red sniffed. 'She just exists because that's all there is for her to do. She's like a wild animal.'

'We ought to take a ride up there wth some provisions after breakfast.' The Kid felt guilty leaving a girl to her fate in such dangerous circumstances.

For the first time since they had encountered the young vixen named Annie Brown they saw interest in her large, tempting eyes.

She struck a match and waited until the fire was roaring in the grate before rising to her full height of five foot nothing.

Her stare made the two men nervous as she moved toward them slowly.

'What's the matter, Annie?' Palomino gazed at her.

'You talk about Winnie?' The ravishing creature moved closer to the seated men. 'Winnie from up on the mountain?'

'Yeah, that's right.' Palomino was curious. 'How do you know of her?'

Annie sat next to the younger partner, sighing.

109

'My mother was a Ute. My pa was a white bear trapper,' she began. 'They knew Winnie's parents. When I was a little girl, I played with Winnie but my mother died from the smallpox. Then Pa came down here and we stayed in town.'

'So you are half-Ute?' Red could feel the warmth of the blazing fire as it heated the room.

'My mother's people are still up on the mountain,' Annie sighed.

'They have been looking after Winnie,' Palomino informed the young girl.

'She is alone?' Annie looked concerned.

'I'm afraid so.' The Kid rubbed his hands together as he felt the circulation returning the blood supply to his fingers.

Annie's head dropped onto her tanned chest.

'I'm all alone now.'

Palomino watched as he saw a tear roll down her cheek, and touched it with his thumb. The flashing eyes sparkled in his direction as she gazed at him.

'Your pa dead?'

'A few months ago,' she answered quietly.

Red Rivers dropped the sheet off his shoulders as he got to his feet. The one thing this grizzly man could not stand was a woman who was crying. It upset him.

'You live in the hotel?'

'Now. But I have a house on the outskirts of town,' she said, getting to her feet.

Kid Palomino watched as she wiped her black,

soot-covered hands on the apron around her waist.
She stood silently beside him as he rose to his feet.
His height made her appear like a doll beside him.
Her head came to just above his elbow.

'Would you like to come up the mountain with me
and Red later on this morning?' He looked down at
her face.

She hesitated once more.

'Why?'

'To see an old friend named Winnie?'

Annie Brown's face started to animate into a smile.
It was glowing with warmth as her fingers touched
Kid Palomino's arm. She headed out of the room.

At the door she paused and stared hard into the
tall man's eyes with gratitude.

'Thank you,' she muttered faintly.

Red watched as she closed the door behind her.
He moved in front of his partner and gave a knowing
look up into the fine-featured man's face.

'We are gonna take a female up the mountain?'

'Yep,' Palomino replied, as he followed his pal to
the warm fire. The heat was penetrating their clothing and taking the frost off their bones.

'Are you crazy?' Red kneeled and tossed another
couple of logs onto the fire. 'That place is bad
enough without a woman tagging along.'

'She could be useful.'

'Explain that.'

'There are Utes up there. Right?'

'Yeah . . .'

111

'She's half-Ute.' Palomino gave a smile. 'Plus, she knows Winnie Patterson.'

'So?'

'Ever heard of insurance, Red?'

Red Rivers pointed at his partner with a look of realization upon his hairy face.

'I get it!'

'Good.' The Kid walked toward the window and stared out at the sun as it rose above the roof-tops.

He was still troubled by the events of a few hours earlier as he leaned against the wooden frame and played with the lace curtains.

'I reckon Matt Davis was truly shocked by the killings earlier, Red.'

'So was I.' Red sat next to the fire and soaked in the heat.

'I mean, he was surprised,' Palomino corrected his friend. 'He had other plans for those men of his. The last thing he would have ordered was their killing.'

'He was choked at the sight of his brother,' Red agreed.

'Whoever killed them four guys is new in town,' the Kid surmised. 'A new gunman has entered Badwater Creek, for a reason we don't yet know.'

'So Matt Davis has enemies. We knew that.'

'Davis has his men burn down a couple of houses because they are sitting on silver deposits,' the Kid thought aloud. 'We put three men in jail. Someone kills not only the three prisoners but also the sheriff. What reason could there be?'

112

'Maybe Matt Davis has a partner he's double-crossed?' Red tossed in his two cents' worth.

Kid Palomino turned and eyed his companion.

'Or Matt Davis has a partner who has just started to double-cross him?'

Red Rivers gave a smile as he looked at his friend from the warmth of the fireplace.

'That sounds probable.'

'It's all we got. So far, anyway.'

Fifteen

The long legs of Dale Cody entered the bank and moved to the caged clerks. His gaunt features seemed to look even paler as he leaned toward the elderly staff.

'Yes, sir?' the old man with the peaked visor asked.

'I have an appointment with Mr Stone,' Cody said, placing a cigar between his teeth and striking a match across the metal cage.

The old clerk coughed as the smoke drifted across his face.

'I'll check with Mr Stone.'

'Do that,' Cody sneered.

'Who shall I say is calling?' The old man seemed too polite to work in a bank. Perhaps he *was* too polite, and that was why he had spent fifty years as a clerk.

'Dale Cody.'

'Take a seat, Mr Cody.' The old man started to waddle away toward the private office area.

Dale Cody just moved up and down the dusty, dark

114

bank foyer, watching the tellers who were watching him.

His expression was hard. There seemed nothing remotely similar to that of a human being behind the thin lidded eyes. He puffed on the cigar without ever touching it as he moved. He touched his moustache as he paced. It was as if he had to keep confirming to himself that it was still there.

After a few tedious minutes he saw the fat figure of Warren Stone standing at the entrance gate that led to the private office.

Dale Cody moved toward the man and then followed him into the office. The two men together were total opposites. One fat, and the other painfully thin.

The other difference between them was that Cody had a Colt Peacemaker hanging from his hip in a stylish holster.

Stone closed the door.

'What are you doing here, Cody?' the fat man asked, as beads of sweat dripped from his chin.

'I'm visiting an old friend.' Cody sat down on the couch.

'This is insane,' Stone fretted.

'I started work this morning,' Cody boasted.

Warren Stone stopped in his tracks and leaned on the desk.

'That was you who killed Bob Davis and—'

'It was.' Cody was proud. 'Four shots. Four dead men. Four bullet holes in four heads. Ain't nobody that can match my marksmanship, Stone.'

Stone managed to make his way to the large padded chair that stood behind the desk. He crawled into the seat and buried his head into his hands.

'You did that?'

'It had to be done.' Cody gave a shrug.

Stone was a very worried man. He tried to smile at the man sitting seven feet away from him, but failed. His lips were shaking in terror and a sudden realization of what was happening in Badwater Creek.

'I don't udnerstand, Cody.'

Dale Cody blew smoke at the fat man and then spat the cigar onto the floor. He watched as it glowed on the floor near the banker's feet.

'Matt Davis is in our way, Stone.' He started to explain his action to the banker. 'I have to get rid of him. He's in our way.'

'But why kill the sheriff and the other men?' Warren Stone looked horrified as he squashed the cigar butt with his heel.

'To kill a spider, it's better to cut off its legs first.' Cody gave a laugh through his gritted teeth. 'Matt Davis is a spider who's losing his legs. One by one I'm cutting them off.'

'You killed those guys because they were Matt Davis' men?'

'Correct, Stone.' Cody grinned again.

Warren Stone seemed glued to his seat as he watched in fearful awe of his new-found partner. He had no idea what he had expected when Cody first approached him with the plan to trick Davis about the silver valuation. Whatever he had expected, this was far, far worse.

The lean man moved toward the banker and held out his hand, as if he wanted Stone to shake it in gratitude.

'What do you want?' Stone questioned the tall slim man with the gun hanging from his hip.

'Give me some greenbacks,' he demanded. 'I need some folding money.'

Stone got to his feet shakily and led the man out of the office and back out into the heart of the bank. Dale Cody went around to the customer side as the manager went to one of the vacant windows.

The only other customer in the bank was the distinctive figure of the Lady G Saloon bartender, Charlie, who was leaning against the wall, filling out a deposit form.

Stone lifted the hatch of the window and leaned over to face the tall man.

'Fifty dollars?' Stone asked.

Dale Cody raised an eyebrow and rubbed his finger along his moustache.

'Make it an even hundred, partner,' he sighed.

'A hundred?' Warren Stone looked at the man for a second, before deciding to comply. 'OK, a hundred.'

'Small bills.' Cody smiled through the serving hatch. 'After all, it's only an even twenty-five bucks per head. Ain't it?'

Charlie's ears pricked up when he overheard the sentence. He looked across at the stranger and then back at the paper slip he was completing. His curiosity had been aroused, and he listened for further information.

Stone counted out the series of bills until he got to one hundred. As he pushed the money through the window he watched the thin hands scoop it up and pat it into shape.

'Thank you.'

'Stay away for a while, Cody,' Stone said, just loud enough for the nearby bartender to overhear.

'Dale Cody aims to please.' The gaunt man tipped his Stetson as he turned and exited the bank.

Charlie watched as the fat figure of Warren Stone returned quickly to his office. Screwing up the paper slip and tossing it into a nearby waste bin, the bartender followed the man out into the street.

Standing on the boardwalk, Charlie looked up and down the quiet street for the distinctive man named Dale Cody. His searching was in vain.

Cody had disappeared into the morning sunshine.

Charlie turned up his collar and ran across the street. He continued running until he reached the Lady G.

He would have to tell his boss, Matt Davis, what he had overheard in the bank. Perhaps Davis might know who Dale Cody was.

Sixteen

It had been a long arduous ride up to the camp of young Winnie Patterson for the three riders. Annie Brown had ridden her hired mount skilfully on the long journey to the clearing below the rock-face. Her prowess with a horse impressed both Kid Palomino and his partner Red Rivers, and they had followed her lead. Her Ute blood and memory had guided them along a trail that few knew even existed.

The three riders sat upon their mounts, watching the long grass sway in the early afternoon breeze.

Annie sat astride the elderly horse, wearing her dress hitched up high, exposing her legs to the elements. The saddle was not designed for a female in a dress, but the young girl had few clothes and none that were correct for equestrian activities.

Her long lashes shaded her dark eyes from the weather as she studied the area for signs of the young Patterson girl.

Then she spotted a bush moving. There were

119

many moving bushes up there on the mountain-top, but this one was different.

Annie's Ute instinct told her that this bush was moving incorrectly. She raised her right arm in its direction, and shouted words in a tongue she had long since thought was forgotten.

Winnie Patterson rose to her feet and gazed at the young, dark-skinned girl sitting on a horse beside the two white men she recognized as Kid Palomino and his partner Red.

Winnie understood the language this girl shouted. It was Ute, like that of her friends.

The Kid, Red and Annie watched as Winnie waded through the tall grass toward them, carrying her ancient rifle.

'Who are you?' Winnie asked Annie as she approached the trio of mounted riders.

Her eyes were locked upon the girl in the saddle. This girl spoke Ute, yet was not dressed like an Indian. Yet her face seemed familiar, and was indeed tanned more than either Palomino's or Red's.

'I am Annie Brown, Winnie.' The beautiful girl smiled down at the dirty female. 'You remember me?'

Winnie just gazed up at the new face. Her eyes seemed to scan every detail of the female above her. There was recognition in her eyes as she watched Annie slide from the saddle onto the ground.

'Annie?' she said softly.

'It has been many years since we last met.'

Palomino and Rivers dismounted and followed the girls as they headed toward the hidden campsite near the rock-face.

Before the Kid could sit down on the awaiting bearskin blanket, the small hands of Winnie Patterson handed him an official-looking envelope with a seal.

Palomino opened the envelope and pulled out the documentation that had spent years in the relative safety of the old wooden chest, she had treasured it so much.

'What is it, Palomino?' Red Rivers asked, rubbing his sparse hair.

'Looks like our pal Winnie is a lady of substantial holdings in Badwater Creek, Red.' The Kid grinned as he surveyed the document.

'What?' Rivers gave his partner a sideways glance.

Kid Palomino waved the document in front of his friend's face, as if fanning away flies.

'This throws a fox in a lot of hen-houses, pal.'

Red turned to the two females, who were sitting down talking intently to one another. He had no idea what his partner was talking about, but then reading had never been his strong point.

Seventeen

Matt Davis stood silently at his office window. He was not looking out at the limited view, but just standing with his eyes open. The thoughts within his tortured mind prevented any real awareness of anything before him.

Regretting things that he had said and done seemed a pointless preoccupation for the sturdy figure who had long turned his back on religious considerations. He had spent too many years considering himself above all laws, to change now.

Yet now, he felt guilty.

Guilty that perhaps somewhere along his own trail he had made a wrong turn. It had cost his only brother his life. It was too late to change now, but he felt the pain of hatred eating into his soul.

It was a pain that sickened him.

He had just been informed by his bartender Charlie about the conversation that had been overheard inside the bank between Dale Cody and Warren Stone.

Davis was grieving over his kid brother and still in a state of shock over the slaughter at the jail. Yet he was aware of the significance of what he had listened to, too.

These were words that normally would have made the man's blood boil, and cause him to take action immediately. The fact that he was still thinking about the information that had been imparted to him made it clear to the hovering bartender that Matt Davis was not his normal self.

The thickly set man moved out of the office and into the sawdust-covered saloon, where he made his way behind the long bar.

The few people who sat quietly drinking around the large room watched as Davis poured himself three fingers of rye.

Not a word was spoken by anyone as they watched the man drink the cheap rot-gut brew. As a rule he would not have touched this brand of cheap rye, leaving it for the customers. Yet he drank it as if it were his private stock.

When Davis poured himself another, everyone's eyes diverted away from him.

Charlie walked behind the bar and moved closer to the man who seemed to be totally confused.

'You OK, Mr Davis?'

'My kid brother and three of my best men have been slaughtered, Charlie,' Davis said quietly. 'Would you be all right in those circumstances?'

Charlie bowed his head and started polishing

glasses. He was beginning to wonder whether he should have said nothing about what he had heard in the bank.

Matt Davis glared across the room at nothing. His eyes were not focused as he sipped the rye.

'A tall man, you say?'

'Thin as a beanpole, boss,' Charlie confirmed.

'What did you say his name was?'

'Cody. Dale Cody,' Charlie said, in a voice that wanted to please the powerful man. 'You know him?'

'The name rings a bell.' Davis finished his drink and picked up the bottle again.

No one had ever seen Matt Davis drunk in all the years he had been in Badwater Creek, but today he was pushing his luck. The third glass went down as fast as the first.

'A tall, thin man named Dale Cody.' Davis mulled the words over as he tried to remember where he had heard the name before. He wondered if it were possible that Warren Stone might have suddenly developed a desire to break free from his influence. Could Stone suddenly have grown a spine?

'He wore a gun that was hung so low on his hip it looked stupid,' Charlie recalled.

Matt Davis stared at his bartender with an expression that displayed a sudden awareness.

'The gun was hung low?' The big man repeated the words and placed his empty glass down on the bar. 'Hung low? Real low?'

'Practically to his knee, boss.' Charlie pointed to

his own thigh to try and show his employer where the holster was on Cody's leg.

'That is low, Charlie.' Davis started to nod as he spoke.

'I never seen a rig like that before.'

'I have.' Davis walked away from the bar and out to the swing-doors of the saloon. He stared out into the cool street and gave a sigh.

'You have?' Charlie was at his employer's heels like a pet dog.

'Only once before.' Davis rubbed his chin as he talked.

'Where?'

'In Cheyenne.' The thickly set man spoke as he remembered the sight in his mind's eye. 'A tall, thin man named Dale Cody was a well-known figure who worked at the assayer's office up there. He had a mean streak. He was also the best man with a Colt I've ever seen.'

'A gunslinger?' Charlie asked.

'Not really, just a man with a gun.' Matt Davis shook his head in frustration. Then he thought for a moment. 'Assayer?'

It suddenly occurred to the burly businessman that he had sent all his remaining gunhands up the mountain to his gold-mine, to blow the place up. That had been before his brother Bob had been gunned down. Stone had said the silver around Badwater Creek was low-grade, according to the assaying report. Dale Cody was many things, but he was also a qualified assayer, Davis brooded.

Matt Davis suddenly felt very alone.

He was very alone.

Could Cody and Stone be in some sort of plot together?

If so, could it have been they who killed Bob and the boys?

The sweat started to run down his face as he focused his eyes on the small undertaker's parlour across the windy street.

Inside that gloomy building four bodies lay in four coffins, and he began to fear he might soon become the fifth.

'Dale Cody,' Davis muttered.

Charlie returned to the bar as his boss continued staring at the undertaker's parlour. It was now clear that his eyes had regained their sight.

Matt Davis had found someone else to transfer his guilt upon.

Eighteen

The small band of Utes suddenly appeared in the clearing upon their highly decorated ponies. Winnie Patterson was the first to notice them, and stood to face the five warriors clad in their leather buckskins.

The five Utes rode slowly toward the quartet of figures who were seated around the small camp-fire.

Kid Palomino swallowed deeply as he watched from his cross-legged position next to Red Rivers and Annie Brown.

Winnie moved to the riders and touched the noses of the first two mounts to greet her. She could see the small band of Utes were troubled by the sight of her guests.

'Little Huntress OK?' the oldest Indian asked as he sat astride his pony, watching the visitors.

'Yes, Lone Eagle.' Winnie looked up at the elegant man with a single feather tied into his black mane. 'These are my friends from below.'

'Who girl?' Lone Eagle pointed his bow at Annie. 'I see her long time ago.'

'She daughter of Ute maiden,' Winnie answered.

The man threw his right leg over his pony's head and slid from the mount.

'She half-Ute?' The warrior asked as he approached the camp-fire.

'You know her from long ago, Lone Eagle,' Winnie confirmed as she walked beside the tall man.

'Stand, girl.' Lone Eagle pointed at Annie. He watched as she stood and then started to grin. He could see who she was. She looked like her mother. 'You are Ute.'

Annie gave a sigh. She did not know whether to be upset or happy by the Indian.

'I am Annie Brown.'

'That your white name.' Lone Eagle gave a belly-laugh. 'You are Small Deer.'

Annie looked around as her companions got to their feet with an expression of surprise.

'What do you mean?' Annie asked.

'Your Ute name means Small Deer,' Winnie explained to her long-lost childhood friend.

Kid Palomino was careful to keep his thumbs tucked into his gunbelt behind the buckle. He did not want to provoke these men into a fight.

'Howdy, Lone Eagle,' the Kid said.

Red touched his hat in greeting and stood close to the tall figure of his partner. He knew that Utes were not known for their hostility toward whites, but was still nervous.

The dark, tanned face of Lone Eagle brooded over the sight of the two white men for a moment. He then concentrated upon the tiny Winnie Patterson, and touched her shoulder.

'Little Huntress must leave here,' he urged.

'Why, Lone Eagle?' she asked, staring up into her friend's face. 'What's wrong?'

'Many men with much dynamite.' Lone Eagle pointed in the direction of the gold-mine belonging to Matt Davis. 'They will blow up mountain.'

'Many men, you say?' Palomino stepped forward and looked into the warrior's face.

'Many men,' Lone Eagle nodded as he pointed again.

'They have dynamite?' Red gulped.

'Much dynamite,' the Ute confirmed.

Kid Palomino rubbed his neck as he hurriedly thought about the men with explosives. Could this be another attempt to get the young Winnie Patterson off the mountain? He pondered about Matt Davis.

'Are they at the mine yet?'

'Not yet.' Lone Eagle made a gesture with his hands. 'But close. very close.'

'Could we get there before them?' the Kid heard himself ask.

'Maybe.' The Indian was doubtful.

'But we might?' Kid Palomino leaned forward eagerly.

'What you thinking about, Kid?' Red Rivers grabbed his partner's arm. 'I hope it ain't what I fear it is.'

'Could we get there before them?' Kid Palomino asked the Ute again.

The proud Indian gave the question a lot of thought, before nodding.

'We go now. We get there first,' Lone Eagle said.

'Then let's get going,' Palomino urged.

Red Rivers looked at the sky as if wondering why the gods always made his young partner do the right thing. Just for once he wished his friend would keep his nose out of other folks' business.

Kid Palomino grabbed the reins of Nugget and mounted the large steed. He pointed at Red.

'Take the girls down the mountain to safety.'

Red Rivers did as he was ordered. He mounted and helped the tiny Winnie Patterson up onto his saddle. She sat behind the rugged man as Annie Brown got onto her own horse. Kid Palomino watched as the two horses rode away down the clearing and disappeared into the forest, taking the three souls with them.

Then he swung Nugget around and followed the five Utes, who were heading for the gold-mine belonging to Matt Davis. They rode hard and fast through the tall grass.

Soon Nugget had drawn level with the five Ute ponies as they all proceeded around the mountain.

Just as they were within sight of the gold-mine

entrance, the shots rang out. An Indian to Palomino's left was plucked from his pony and crashed into the soft grass. All five remaining riders pulled their mounts to a halt and dismounted quickly.

Palomino had his trusty Winchester in hand as he fell into the cover of the tall grass. His companions only had bows and arrows, but he felt that they would probably be just as effective.

The firing continued as Kid Palomino crawled toward the closely grouped Utes.

'Men over there.' Lone Eagle pointed to the tree-edged ridge to their right.

The Kid gave a deep sigh and, after removing his Stetson raised his head to peer in the direction that Lone Eagle was indicating. A volley of shots followed, forcing him to duck quickly. The bullets bouncing off the mountain rock-face behind them sent deafening echoes across the area.

'How many men, Lone Eagle?' Palomino asked the warrior who was lying on his side with an arrow already in his bow.

The Ute placed his bow on the grass and raised both hands, showing eight fingers.

The Kid rolled his eyes.

'Eight?' he muttered, as a further volley of firing headed in their direction. This time it was closer than before. Too close.

The Kid waved his arm for his associates to fan out through the tall grass. He wanted them to separate and make smaller targets for Matt Davis' gang. The Utes obeyed, and soon he was unable to see any of them himself.

Now it was up to him to lead the crawl.

Head on.

Palomino crawled ahead, clutching the rifle in his sweaty grip, before he got to a protruding rock. It was only about three feet high and probably less in width, but he used it for cover.

Cranking the rifle, he swiftly got onto his knees and started firing at the men he could see below him. They were using the trees for cover. It was an effective strategy for most of them.

Most, but not all.

Two of the men were soon picked off by Kid Palomino's accuracy with the long Winchester, but the majority soon realized from where the fatal bullets were coming.

Johnson, Matt Davis' top man, signalled the five remaining men to move wider around through the trees. Then the arrows started to fly in. Another of Johnson's men fell, then another. This was not what he had expected.

The Utes were spaced out in the tall grass very wide apart. So wide apart that the normally cool gunhand was reduced to kneeling in terror. Johnson was fumbling his bullets into the six-gun as an arrow ripped into his side. The heat raged through his body as he fell onto his face.

Seeing Johnson felled by an arrow, the remaining

few men started to scramble for their horses. The pack-mule was starting to get troubled by the activities around him and was bucking wildly.

The sticks of dynamite began to fall from the boxes strapped to its back. Then Kid Palomino found his chosen target, and hit the pack upon the back of the irate animal with a quickly delivered volley of rifle shots.

The ensuing explosion was thunderous, and caused a flash of vivid white light to blind the Kid temporarily. The black cloud of smoke rose like an animated mushroom, with an inferno at its base. Trees raged in burning fury around the area. None of the gunmen had survived the earth-shaking blast.

A wave of debris erupted out of the edge of the forest, covering the four secreted Utes and Kid Palomino. Tree remnants, mixed with a sickly concentrate of human and animal flesh, rained down for minutes after the original eruption.

Lone Eagle was the first to rise to his feet when the air cleared.

His stony expression was apparently unmoved by the scene of carnage before him. To him it was a victory for the Little Huntress. The other Ute braves soon appeared up from their hiding-places. Two of them went back to find the wounded friend who had been shot from his pony only minutes earlier.

Kid Palomino struggled to his feet, plucking his hat from the grass and hitting it against his leg several times. He was aware that many men had died at his hands this day. It was not a thought he could dwell upon too long.

The Utes followed the tall white man silently to their awaiting mounts. Lone Eagle watched as the quiet man slid his rifle into its long holster on the saddle of the large stallion, and gathered up the long reins.

'You are good man,' Lone Eagle said to Kid Palomino as he rested his head against the large honey-coloured horse.

Kid Palomino turned and stared at the warrior.

'That was bad, Lone Eagle. Real bad.'

'Killing never good,' the Indian agreed, as his friends helped their wounded companion to his waiting pony.

'Never is. You're right,' the Kid nodded.

They all mounted. Palomino held his reins tightly and turned the large horse around.

'You take your friend to my partner Red. He'll tend his wound mighty fine,' the Kid said, looking down the trail that Annie Brown had shown to them. 'Tell Red to follow me back to town when he's done.'

'You go?' Lone Eagle enquired.

'I gotta get to town,' Palomino replied. 'I think I might be needed there.'

The small band of Utes watched as the rider spurred his horse and rode down the grass-covered slope, before disappearing into the thick wall of trees.

Whatever reason this man on the fine horse had for heading off so quickly, the Indians could only guess at it.

Lone Eagle led his tiny band to where they knew Winnie Patterson would be waiting with her two friends.

Nineteen

It had been a very long time since Matt Davis had strapped on his six-shooters. So long that he had to clean the pistols before loading them with the cartridges from his virginal gunbelt.

He was no gunfighter, and never had been.

This was a man who had always hired others to do his killing for him. Yet now, he was preparing to use his guns.

The sound of the far-off explosion up high in the mountains had given him artificial confidence. Wrongly thinking his men had achieved their goal, he was going to have it out with the double-dealing Warren Stone.

Matt Davis practised with his weapons in the seclusion of his office at the back of the Lady G.

He was confident that Johnson would soon return with the rest of the gang and that they would tackle Dale Cody for him.

All he had to do was go to the bank and confront his long-time partner in crime. He knew that the fat

Stone had tricked him, but he had to face the man and ask him whether or not he had sent the evil Cody to kill his brother Bob and the three other members of his gang.

Being able to pull his guns from his holsters at a reasonable speed gave Matt Davis courage. He grabbed his hat from the stand and pulled it on. Then, pushing his long coat tails over the white handles of his weapons, he strode from his office.

Charlie the bartender stood motionless behind the bar as he watched his employer pace across the saloon and out into the cold street.

Davis stood for an instant on the boardwalk and heaved in a large lungful of air, before proceeding toward the bank.

The few townsfolk who were out in the afternoon breeze stopped and watched as the solid man strode down the centre of main street toward his destination.

Unblinking, Davis marched like a soldier to the bank. Each step firmer than the previous one. One by one the people in the street seemed to disappear, as if knowing that soon lead would be flying.

Matt Davis mounted the opposite boardwalk and continued toward the large building where he knew the obese Warren Stone would be waiting. Each step seemed to bring him further rage. Each step made him angrier.

Entering the dim interior of the bank, Davis paused for a few moments as if allowing his eyes to adjust to the difference in light. Then he renewed his quest and walked up to the locked gate that was the only defence for the elderly tellers. Beyond lay the door to Stone's office. An office he had been in many times previously.

Now the door seemed to heckle at him in his imagination.

Pulling out both pistols he shot the lock off the gate and kicked the wooden structure down.

Davis recommenced to the door and kicked that open as well, before entering the solid room.

Warren Stone stood next to his chair shaking like a man who knew his life was in mortal danger. His face was soaked in perspiration as he made his way around the desk, fearfully staring at Matt Davis and the two guns in his hands.

'What you want, Matt?' Stone managed to say.

Davis walked toward the pig of a human being and gazed at him with eyes that were red with fury.

'Answers, Stone,' he snarled, pushing both barrels into the man's large middle. 'Answers.'

'To what?' Stone bluffed.

'Dale Cody?' Davis pushed his prey backward and watched him stumble onto the desk, sending inkwells and papers cascading everywhere. 'The worthless silver? My brother?'

Warren Stone stopped himself from tumbling onto the floor before standing upright once more.

It was a useless act, as he found out when Matt Davis kicked his short legs from under him. The banker landed upon the floor heavily and found himself crawling around the desk, back to his padded chair.

'I don't understand, Matt.'

'You lying dog,' Davis growled at the gasping man who was clinging to the chair.

'I have no idea what you're talking about!' Stone continued his denial.

'You do. If you keep lying I'm gonna blow your brains out.'

Warren Stone dragged himself up onto the chair and panted as he tried in vain to get his wind back.

'You are upset because of the shootings, Matt.'

Davis raised a pistol and aimed at Stone's left hand. Then he squeezed the trigger and shot a hole through the centre of the plump object. Stone reeled in agony as he realized what had just happened.

'I got plenty more bullets left, Stone,' Davis grinned.

'No . . . no.' Stone raised his bleeding hand before his face in defeat. 'You win. You win.'

'You gonna tell me the truth?'

'Yes. Yes. Yes.' Stone grabbed the desk and tried to steady himself. 'I'll tell you everything. Everything.'

'Start talking.' Matt Davis hovered, holding the guns firmly in his large hands.

'It was Cody. When I got him to assay the silver he came to me and said he had a plan to outwit you.' Stone cried as he spoke the words. 'He said it was top grade silver ore, but he would write a false

139

certificate for it. To make you believe it wasn't worth collecting.'

'Didn't he figure I'd find out?' Davis asked coldly.

'He said he didn't care if you did,' Stone sobbed, as he watched the blood flowing from his hand.

'Didn't care?'

'He's crazy.' Stone shook his head, looking down. 'He ain't scared of anyone.'

'Was it his idea to kill my brother and my men?' Davis was getting furious at the thought of anyone being that cold-blooded.

'I had no idea that was gonna happen, Matt. Honestly.'

'Where's Mr Cody holed up, Stone?'

Stone suddenly realized he had no idea where the ruthless Dale Cody was hiding.

'I don't know.'

Davis raised his guns again and squared them at the banker's face. He watched the fat man shrug and look away from the barrels. Then he lowered the weapons to his side slowly.

'I believe you, Stone,' he heard himself say as he exited the office and strolled back into the street. He knew that he could have killed the man, but knew that it would have served no purpose. Stone had been so scared he couldn't have lied whilst staring down the barrels of his guns.

Dale Cody was somewhere close. But where? He walked along the empty boardwalk, still holding on to the pistols. He was staring at every building, trying

140

to see the tall thin man with the thin moustache and the gun.

A gun hung low. Real low.

The man walked the entire length of the long street until he got to the hotel. He entered and moved toward the desk.

Frank Giles looked up to see Matt Davis heading straight at him, with the two guns gripped firmly in his hands. He felt like running, but his legs refused to move from the spot.

'Mr Davis?' Frank stammered, with a half-smile on his face. He now knew where the gunshot he had heard had come from. It had come from one of the pistols in the man's hands before him.

'Let me see the register, Frank,' Davis snapped.

Giles turned the thick book around and watched as the brooding man studied the names. A glimmer of a smile etched itself on Davis' face, as he saw what he was searching for.

Dale Cody, Cheyenne.

Davis pointed with the barrel of one of his guns at the name. 'Is this critter in?'

Frank Giles turned his head to read the name on the wide page of the register.

'Mr Cody is out, Mr Davis.'

'Where?'

'I have no idea.' Giles had a strained expression. 'He only checked in a couple of hours ago, and left straight away.'

Matt Davis nodded.

'Thanks, Frank.'

The terrified man watched as the owner of The Lady G Saloon walked quietly out of the foyer, back out into the street.

The dust was blowing down the empty street as the burly man started to cross toward the saloon.

He had only managed to get halfway across, when a voice echoed around him and the words swirled in the wind.

'Looking for me, Davis?'

Matt Davis stopped and looked all about him. He could not tell where the voice had originated due to the breeze.

'Davis! What's wrong, Davis?'

Matt Davis held both his guns out as he turned slowly, like a cat trying to catch its own tail. Then he spotted the shooting-rig.

The shooting rig that was hung real low on the slim leg of Dale Cody. The tall man was leaning casually against a wooden upright, next to the undertaker's parlour.

Davis started to move hesitatingly toward the thin, gaunt man, who just leaned and stared.

'You're Cody!' he shouted over the windy breeze.

'That is my handle, Davis,' Cody answered, without bothering to move from his position. He simply continued to lean against the pole.

Step by step the big man approached his quarry, clutching the heavy six-guns in his sweating hands. Each step seemed to bring an even greater degree of distaste upon Dale Cody's face. The thin man permitted Matt Davis to get within twenty paces from whence he waited, before easing himself upright.

The glare from the thin, hooded eyes seemed to stop the saloon-owner in his tracks.

Davis stood silently, holding the guns at his side. This was not a man to try and outdraw, he thought. Cody was evil in a narrow suit.

'Feeling brave, Mr Davis?' the man from Cheyenne asked, as he stepped down from the boardwalk onto the firm soil.

'Was it you?' Davis shouted at the slender vermin before him. 'Was it you who killed my brother?'

Dale Cody started to laugh.

It was not the sort of laugh anyone who heard it could easily forget. It had a chilling effect upon Davis as the two men circled each other, Davis still holding his two pistols tightly in his hands, Cody seemingly unconcerned by the sight, still allowing his gun to rest in its low-hung holster. The laughing continued. Now it seemed like the sound of mocking.

'Answer me, Cody,' Davis demanded.

'Who was your brother again?' Cody enquired, as his long legs slowly paced in a circle around the sturdy man.

Matt Davis raised his weapons and aimed them at the slim figure who continued to walk around him in the middle of the empty street. Even this did nothing to worry the tall man.

'My brother was the sheriff!' Davis yelled.

143

'The sheriff. . .?' Cody paused for a second, before continuing his slow march. 'Yes, I did kill him, Mr Davis.'

Matt Davis had never seen such a cold-blooded man in all his days. He had thought of himself as being ruthless, but compared to Dale Cody he was almost a saint.

'Why?' Davis snarled, having constantly to move to his left to keep his guns trained upon the angular form. 'Why did you kill him?'

'He happened to be there,' Cody smiled.

'What?'

'I went to kill the three gunmen in the jail, Davis.' Cody did not even seem to be looking at Matt Davis as he talked and walked. 'Your brother just happened to be there as well.'

'The three men in the cell were unarmed, Cody.' Davis could not believe that anyone could brag about killing unarmed men.

Dale Cody glanced at Davis with a smile on his thin lips.

'That made it even better.'

'Better?'

'It was fun.' Cody started to laugh again. 'A lot more fun than if they had been armed.'

Matt Davis had heard enough.

The laughter was echoing inside his skull.

The sound was making him feel sick.

He elevated his pistols and began to start firing at the gaunt figure.

144

Somehow, Dave Cody had drawn his Colt from the low holster and fired just one shot. One single shot as the bullets passed by him.

The thickly set Matt Davis seemed to keel over backwards, with his guns still firing heavenward.

Cody stood sideways-on to his victim for a moment, before turning his boots in the direction of Matt Davis' prostrate body, lying on his back in the street.

Five long-legged paces brought him to the head of the big man, and Dale Cody stared triumphantly down. The single bullet-hole was high in the centre of the forehead of Matt Davis.

Dale Cody slid his still-smoking Colt into the holster, before leaving the scene.

Many eyes in many windows watched the thin man as he headed back toward the hotel. The pace was deliberate. Just like the man himself.

Twenty

If Dale Cody had walked just a fraction faster from the body of his latest victim, he might have entered the hotel before seeing the rider who approached.

He did see the approaching rider though. This was a man that he had studied for the past couple of days in Badwater Creek, and, although Kid Palomino had nothing to do with his plan, his mere presence seemed to infuriate Cody.

The thin man hesitated, as Kid Palomino rode Nugget past him and stopped at the dead form of Matt Davis.

The Kid dismounted and pushed his mount away. He knelt down beside the dead man on the ground.

The bullet-hole in the head was almost like a trademark for the killer. Blood trickled down into the ground from the wound, as Palomino realized the shots he had heard as he had been racing to town had resulted in this man's demise.

The undertaker came cautiously out of his parlour, and up to where Palomino was kneeling.

The Kid looked up into the elderly man's face. It was a face that seemed to reflect death. It was a face of white and grey. If blood still circulated in this man's body it didn't show.

'Who did this, mister?' Kid Palomino asked, as the old man bent over the body. 'Who killed Matt Davis?'

The undertaker did not speak. His eyes glanced up the street toward the hotel, at the tall, thin man who stood watching them.

It was clear to the Kid what the old-timer was indicating.

'The thin dude?' he asked.

The undertaker seemed to blink his reply.

'Thanks.' Palomino got to his feet and turned toward the far-off figure. 'Any idea who he is?'

'Dale Cody from Cheyenne,' the man from the morgue replied quietly behind him.

'Thanks.' Kid Palomino started to walk back up the street toward the lean-looking form.

Dale Cody was a name he had heard of in his days as a lawman down south. As he gained on the man, he began to recall the gossip about the man with the gun that was hung way down on his thigh.

Palomino's eyes focused in on Cody's shooting-rig, and he began to feel uneasy. He kept on walking toward the man who seemed to be too thin to be still living.

He remembered the stories of the man who was so fast and so accurate with his single gun, he seldom if ever needed to waste two bullets on one target.

Kid Palomino's neck hair started to tingle as he closed in on the watchful Dale Cody.

This was a man who was fast.

Probably too fast.

He kept heading for the man. Pride had suddenly taken over his emotions. The sane thing to do would have been to keep away from such a man. A man who could kill with a single shot. A man who had fired four times and killed four men in a matter of seconds was no mere gunslinger. This man was more of a marksman.

The two men's eyes had now locked together as Palomino slowed to a halt. They were now standing sixteen paces apart.

Cody had turned his body sideways-on, making him an even narrower target than normal.

Kid Palomino stared at the man.

'You kill that man back there?'

'I certainly did,' Dale Cody boasted, holding his hands together on his chest as if praying. 'Matt Davis deserved it.'

'Why did you do that?' The Kid was not sure it was the sensible thing to do, but he kept asking questions. 'Why did you gun Davis down?'

'He fired first.' Cody seemed to be watching Kid Palomino from the corner of his eye.

'But why did he fire first?'

'I guess he felt lucky.' Cody giggled for a moment, before regaining his composure.

Kid Palomino rubbed his face with his left hand.

He had squared up to many men, but this was the first time he felt as if he was not going to come out on top. The thought of this man being able to place a bullet between his eyes made him very uneasy.

'You killed the four men in the jail last night?'

'Another one of my moments of weakness, Mr Kid Palomino.'

'You know me?' The Kid was now sweating.

'I know a lot of things.' Dale Cody started to pace slowly in a circle around the worried figure of Kid Palomino.

Palomino gazed at the ground as the man walked about him like a buzzard over a dead body.

'You have to kill all these folks?'

'Why not, Kid?' Cody started to laugh at a joke to which only he knew the punch line. 'Killing is sometimes required.'

'Required?'

'To end a period of time.' Dale Cody was not a man to try to understand logic. He had a rule-book in his soul that was different from any normal man.

'I think you have got the better of me, Cody,' Palomino admitted as he watched the man continuing his pacing.

'What do you mean?'

'I reckon you might not be faster than me, but you seem to be able to hit whatever you're aiming at.' The Kid sighed. 'I can fire off a lot of bullets in the right direction but how many would hit the target?'

'You have two Colts to my one, Kid.' Cody smiled as he walked. 'That must even things up a bit.'

Kid Palomino listened to the words, but was not convinced by them. He stood squarely, facing down the street, trying to ignore the man who was walking around him. In the distance he could see the undertaker being assisted by a couple of men, hauling Matt Davis' body into the parlour. Then he concentrated on Dale Cody, who was walking between himself and the far-off undertakers.

'Quit walking around, Cody,' Palomino snapped.

The thin man was surprised by the outburst, and ceased his moving.

'My, my, my. I do think the famous Kid Palomino is worried by Dale Cody.'

Palomino stared at the man ahead of him.

'I could walk away, Cody,' he began. 'I ain't the sheriff in this little town. I could get on my horse and ride. But I've been a lawman for most of my days and even though I ain't wearing a badge right now, it's kinda my duty to face up to you. I don't have any idea why you done what you done, but I know it's wrong. You killed three men in a jail. Just gunned them down. The sheriff might have drawn on you, and lost, but the guys in the cell were unarmed. Yep, I could ride, and nobody would be any wiser. Except you and me. That's two men too many.'

'Ride, Palomino.' Dale Cody gestured to the far-away Nugget, who waited down the street. 'I'll let you ride.'

150

'Like I said, it's my duty to square up to you because I'm the only one who can. There ain't nobody else left. Only me.' The Kid was sweating as he lowered his hands over the matched Colt Peacemakers in his hand-tooled gunbelt.

'You're scared, Kid.' Dale Cody did not realize just how scared his opponent was.

'You're right, Cody,' Palomino said through his gritted teeth, as he watched the thin, gaunt gunslinger turn to face him. 'I seen what your victims look like. I guess the odds of my ending up as just another notch on your gun-handle are greater than my winning this fight. But I ain't riding away.'

Cody was confused. He had never before met a man who admitted that he was unlikely to be the conqueror of a duel. Yet, even knowing that he was probably going to die for no reason at all that made any sense, this man refused to back off.

'You want to die, Kid?'

'Not much.'

'Then why face up to me?'

'Someone has to stop you.'

The two men glared at each other for a long time. Both not sure why they were risking their lives. Both convinced they were in the right.

The hands flexed as they strained above the handles of their pistols. Sweat trickled down the faces of both men as they stared deeply into each other's eyes. The stares so hard that both men were burning each other's souls with the intensity of the concentration required. The first man to blink was usually the loser in these matters.

Neither the Kid nor Cody were about to blink and lose sight of the other for even a hundredth of a second. Both men just locked onto each other's pupils and glared. The two men started to go for their irons, and it was Dale Cody who managed to get his Colt from the low-hung holster first.

Then, as if from heaven, a noise.

Behind the startled Dale Cody came a sound that echoed.

A loud, ringing sound.

For a split-second, the lethal gunslinger was distracted enough to glance backwards over his shoulder.

That was all it took for Kid Palomino to drop to his knees, draw both guns and fire. A fraction of a second prior to his firing, a single bullet from Cody's pistol had passed above his head, nicking the top of his Stetson.

An exhausted Kid Palomino watched as the evil gunman fell backward into the dirt of the street. Dale Cody was quite dead. Not killed with the accuracy of a single shot to the head, but by two well-placed bullets to the chest.

The sound that had saved Kid Palomino's life rang out once more. Kid Palomino lay in the dirt, listening to the church bells as they vibrated around the wooden buildings. He gazed down the long street at the small, white-washed building with the large wooden cross nailed to its short spire, and closed his eyes in thanks.

It suddenly occurred to Palomino; it must be Sunday.

Finale

The past few days had been quiet and uncommonly peaceful for Badwater Creek and its citizens.

The undertaker had been seen smiling after his most profitable week since starting up in business forty years earlier.

It seemed the time was right for the two men called Red Rivers and Kid Palomino to think about heading on.

After Marshal Dobbs had arrived at 2.30 on the noon stage, they had informed him of everything that was going on in Badwater.

They knew that this experienced law officer would soon get this small town straightened out, and felt confident as they left the silver-haired man in the sheriff's office.

Confident that law had at last reached this small corner of the Colorado territory. Confident that Marshal Dobbs would sort everything out in his usual honest manner.

Annie Brown had returned to town with Red

Rivers late on Sunday afternoon, and was back work-ing at her job in the hotel.

The two men had gathered up their few posses-sions in their saddle-bags and checked out of the hotel. Sitting on the hitching-rail outside the dusty building, they were giving the place a long, last look.

Something was still bothering the taller, younger man as they watched the stagecoach having a fresh team attached.

Kid Palomino knew that he had at least one thing left to do before leaving town.

'Shall I go get the horses from the livery, Kid?' the red-haired man asked.

'Yeah,' the Kid nodded, getting to his feet. 'Pick up some provisions as well.'

Red touched his battered hat and jumped down into the sun-drenched street. The wind was still cooler than he liked, but he was resigned to the fact that it would probably get colder before it got warmer.

'You gonna see that Lucy lady?' The bearded man smiled as he headed away.

'Just get some beans and jerky, Red,' Palomino muttered as he headed off toward the house of Doc Jenkins.

As he raised his knuckles to knock on the door-frame, the small wife of the old doctor opened the door. Her smile greeted him warmly.

'Come on in.' She led the way back to the familiar room.

The tall Kid cupped his Stetson in his hands and moved toward the seated figure of Lucy Hall, who was wrapped in her white robe on the padded chair.

As Palomino sat next to her he gave the attractive woman a fond look.

'Marshal Dobbs will look after you and sort out your claim for the silver on your property, Lucy.'

'Who is he?'

'A good man. An honest man,' Palomino said, staring at the rug at his feet.

'Does that mean you're leaving?' Her face was frozen as she bit her lip.

'Yep.' He felt sad as he rose back to his feet.

Her small hand held his for a moment as he hesitated. His glance spoke words that he could never utter.

'I ain't never seen a lady that looked so much like an angel, Lucy.' His voice shook with emotion as he spoke. 'But I'm just a cowboy, and cowboys ain't suited for angels.'

'You take care of yourself.' Lucy Hall seemed to be giving the handsome man a command.

'I'll try, ma'am.'

She released her grip reluctantly and watched as he slowly left the room, then the house. The air in the room seemed to get colder after he had gone. It might have been the breeze that had blown into the house, but Lucy Hall doubted it.

Tears rolled down her cheeks.

Outside the house, the muscular man returned his

156

Stetson onto his head and tried to shield his eyes from onlookers.

A few minutes later he saw Red riding Derby toward him, leading the magnificent Nugget. The older man brought his mount to a stop outside the doctor's home, and watched as his partner slowly got into his saddle.

'You OK?' Red asked, passing the reins to the younger man.

'Yep,' Palomino lied.

At that moment, the two men saw a sight that they had never considered possible. Riding slowly into town on a painted pony, Winnie Patterson, the 'Little Huntress' was leading a small band of Utes. Lone Eagle rode close to her as if he were her protector from all things dangerous.

The unusual band paused their ponies next to Red Rivers and the Kid for a moment.

'We come as you tell us to come,' Lone Eagle said bluntly to the two men.

Winnie sat on her pony, watching the townspeople who were in turn watching them. Hanging over the pony's neck was a leather bag full of heavy ore. Gold ore.

'Why we have to come to town, pretty man?' Winnie asked the Kid.

'Because that paper you gave me was a deed, Winnie,' Palomino explained. 'You own half the land around here. Your father might have been a mountain man and gold prospector, but he was also a real

157

smart fella. He bought half this valley when there wasn't even a town here.'

'Does that mean she is owed a lot of rent?' Red smiled.

'It sure does.' Palomino smiled and pointed down the street, toward the sheriff's office. 'Down there is a man with a silver badge. He'll sort everything out for you.'

Winnie was still confused as she kicked the pony on and rode off down the street with her faithful friends in tow. She had no idea that from this day forth her life would change for ever.

The people who watched as she rode before the small band of proud Utes had no idea that their lives would also change.

This young unwashed female was the wealthiest person that any of them would ever set eyes upon, however long they lived.

Red Rivers also watched as Winnie made her innocent way along toward the jail, before turning back to his partner. The wind was starting to blow hard again.

'I guess we are now on our way to Wyoming?'

'Nope. Texas,' the Kid corrected, as he stood in his stirrups and allowed the large stallion his head.

With a howl of satisfied delight the two riders waved their hats in the air as they let their mounts gallop. They were off to find a sun with some heat in it.